D1740199

A WHIRLWIND ROMANCE

Whitney had worked in the small bookshop in Melbourne, Australia, for several years. She was still reeling from the news that the owner had decided to sell up when handsome Zach Chandler called in to collect some rare books. Zach asked Whitney out and they soon fell in love. However, their backgrounds were very different — she came from a humble family and his was fabulously rich. Could their love survive the many obstacles this would throw in their path?

NOELENE JENKINSON

A WHIRLWIND ROMANCE

Complete and Unabridged

LINFORD
Leicester

First published in Great Britain in 2002

First Linford Edition
published 2003

British Library CIP Data

Jenkinson, Noelene
A whirlwind romance.—Large print ed.—
Linford romance library
1. Love stories
2. Large type books
I. Title
823.9'14 [F]

ISBN 0–7089–4926–6

Published by
F. A. Thorpe (Publishing)
Anstey, Leicestershire

Set by Words & Graphics Ltd.
Anstey, Leicestershire
Printed and bound in Great Britain by
T. J. International Ltd., Padstow, Cornwall

This book is printed on acid-free paper

1

Wow,' Tess exclaimed. 'You should see this guy getting off the tram. He's gorgeous. I wonder if he's married?'

From the stepladder between rows of shelves where she juggled a stack of books, Whitney Leighton glanced down at her assistant, peering out on to a wet, windswept Melbourne street. It was September and officially spring but winter wouldn't release its chilly grasp this year. The lovely southern capital of Victoria situated on the banks of the Yarra River and the second largest city in Australia, had been awash for weeks.

Intrigued by the girl's enthusiasm, Whitney glanced out of the bookshop window. She caught a flash of dark hair and an expensive suit, and sighed. She didn't have time to waste on some silver-spooned Adonis. Her mind still reeled over the bombshell dear old Mrs

Pearce had dropped last Friday night. She wanted to sell Bygone Books and retire to tropical Queensland.

Whitney had thought it would be years before the still-lively seventy-year-old considered retirement, time Whitney desperately needed to build her meagre savings if she had any hope of buying the business.

Mrs Pearce had just invested in a new computer system to transfer and maintain all their stock on to a database, apparently with the sale of the bookshop in mind. And that meant Whitney was working nights and weekends keyboarding thousands of books on to the specially-designed computer software.

Brooding over her dilemma all weekend had proved fruitless because here it was Monday morning and she was still no closer to a solution. Whitney shook her head and grinned.

'Close your mouth, Tess. It's rude to stare.'

Suddenly, the young woman gasped.

'Oh, my goodness. He's coming in here!'

'Then he's all yours.'

Whitney climbed higher to reach the upper shelves, her mind once more plunged into serious contemplation. Four weeks! How could Mrs Pearce do this to her? Whitney scowled. Without the bookshop, she would be unemployed and homeless. There were no guarantees a new owner would retain the staff or allow her to remain in the upstairs flat.

Living alone was exorbitant in any city these days, even if she shared. A move to the suburbs with her mother, or outback South Australia with her father, was feasible but unlikely. She had lived independently of her parents for a decade and intended to remain so.

She could ask the banks for a loan but, with little money and no assets for collateral, she was not naïve about the reality of her prospects. Whitney's gaze swept the small, crammed store into which, as manager in recent years, she had poured all her time and love.

The doorbell jingled and a gust of damp air blew in the open door from elegant Collins Street with their first customer for the week. Whitney glanced toward the new arrival. He stared at her and, caught off guard, she teetered on the steps. Tess had been right. Close up, he certainly was a dreamboat, with good looks, easy manner and thick dark hair, beaded with raindrops.

Transfixed, Whitney gaped back, trapped by his lethal smile. He broke their gaze and turned to Tess.

'Zach Chandler. You're holding two books for me.'

Whitney instantly recognised the deep, smooth voice from his telephone call last week.

Tess turned to her superior for help, and Whitney descended the ladder and off-loaded the armful of books on to her assistant who darted Whitney a rueful grimace and disappeared from sight. Whitney turned to the customer, forcing herself to look into a pair of clear grey eyes that twinkled back at her with softness and warmth.

'Good morning, Mr Chandler. I have them ready.'

Diverting her gaze, she reached beneath the counter and retrieved a wrapped parcel of books, slipping them into a carry bag. As he handed her his gold credit card, their fingers brushed. Feeling as if she had been hit by a current of electricity, Whitney drew in a sharp breath and practised a casual business smile.

'You were fortunate to find these,' she babbled. 'Our buyer only acquired them two weeks ago. They're extremely rare.'

Whitney scanned his card, completed the transaction and handed it back. Inevitably, their gazes met again and held.

'My brother-in-law is a collector. He'll appreciate them.'

He paused and leaned closer.

'You're incredibly attractive.'

Taken aback, Whitney blushed.

'Thank you.'

'Come out with me tonight?'

Zach wasn't entirely sure what compulsion urged him to ask. Had it been the crystal blue eyes that entranced him? The lovely wide mouth? Maybe it was the thick, luxurious copper hair. Probably it was all of those reasons and more but mostly it was that flash of attraction and her genuine appealing honesty that fascinated him. In his world, such a characteristic was rare and precious. Astonished by his audacity, even allowing herself to be flattered by it, Whitney laughed self-consciously.

'No,' she replied.

'You won't reconsider?'

She shook her head and heard a background cough from Tess, out of sight but obviously not out of hearing. He produced a business card.

'When you change your mind, call me.'

'I won't.'

He pushed the card towards her.

'Maybe you will,' he said softly.

With a self-confident, departing smile and wicked wink, he opened the door and was gone. To the dying echoes of the doorbell, Whitney watched him join a stream of hurrying pedestrians in the misty rain and stride away with powerful grace until lost from sight.

Tess reappeared, a hand over her heart, her eyes glazed with awe.

'That was so romantic!'

'Forward, you mean,' Whitney scoffed.

'You refused him. You didn't even consider a date with him.'

Tess looked desolate. She sneezed, snatched a tissue from the box on the counter and blew her nose.

'In between eavesdropping,' Whitney said and changed the subject, 'did you manage to finish those books?'

Tess pulled a face and nodded, then sneezed again.

'Then let's get back to work,' Whitney said in a business-like manner.

For a while, Zachary Chandler's business card sat neglected on the counter until Whitney could no longer resist the temptation. Feeling guilty and weak, she picked it up and read it. Her eyebrows rose. A stockbroker. The irony was not lost on her. The Stock Exchange building was only blocks away along Collins Street. The useless hope crossed her mind that she might even see him again. He knew she was here.

Within the hour, an extravagant bouquet of ivory roses was delivered to the shop. Whitney assumed someone had made a mistake, until she read the card. Zachary Chandler! Her heart raced with secret pleasure until she wondered if he bombarded all women he met like this after five minutes' acquaintance. He was a charming and smooth operator.

But the roses were only the beginning! Every hour for the rest of the day, more flowers appeared. Tess squealed and Whitney groaned. He was mad but they were lovely. Whitney grew desperate for places to put them.

She should telephone the persistent

Mr Chandler, thank him and ask him to stop. He had proved his point. She hadn't forgotten him. His secretary had probably ordered them anyway, Whitney thought wryly.

By late afternoon, she realised the flowers had to go. Tess continually coughed and sneezed, and her eyes were red and watery.

'It's only a chill. It's this changeable, spring weather,' the long-suffering girl protested.

'You could be allergic. I'll whip the flowers upstairs just in case.'

Whitney covered tables, dressers and cupboards in the flat with vases then insisted Tess leave early. Whitney worked late, until she heard her flatmate, Maz, clomping up the outside stairs. She bolted the shop, turned the OPEN sign around to CLOSED and ran upstairs to join her.

'What's all this, then?' Maz demanded.

Shocking orange hair reflected the trendy hairdresser's vibrant personality as she stood in the centre of their flower-filled sitting-room. Her hands were planted on her hips and her dark eyes flashed with mischief.

'Who is Zach? Where did you meet? How long have you known him?'

Whitney sank on to the sofa, kicked off her shoes and counted off the answers with her fingers.

'A stockbroker. In the shop.' She checked her watch. 'Eight hours ago.'

Maz moved over to the ivory roses, plunged her nose against the velvet petals and inhaled deeply.

'Has he asked you out?'

'Pretty much his first question.'

Maz grinned.

'Cool. Where's he taking you?'

'He's not.'

'Whitney, you rarely date. You work too hard. Then a guy falls into your lap and you refuse him?'

She sat down beside Whitney, crossed her legs and rested her elbows on her knees.

'This man sounds, like, to die for. Where's the problem?'

Whitney shrugged, fiddling with the tassels on the sofa cushion she hugged and remembered a pair of warm grey eyes.

'I have other things on my mind right now, remember? Like a roof over our heads and a job.'

Maz shook her head and her short curls bounced.

'Then a date is exactly what you need.'

'I spoke to the man for less than five minutes. I thought he was just flirting. He came on so strong and fast.'

And although she wouldn't admit it, she had been swept up by its force.

'It's Kismet,' Maz enthused. 'Fate. Go for it!'

Whitney grinned at her friend's exuberance.

'What does a rich guy like that want with a working girl like me?'

'Don't analyse him to death. Just say yes. He's probably your soul mate or something but you'll never know if you don't go out with him.'

Maz uncurled herself and rose.

'Now, let's eat. I've got gym at eight.'

Alone later, as Whitney watered her flowers, the telephone rang. Absently, she answered it. Her heartbeat stepped up a pace at the familiar, warm voice on the other end.

'Changed your mind yet?'

'Not really.'

'I detect a trace of uncertainty. Flowers help?'

She stifled a grin.

'They were thoughtful but excessive.'

'Do you have a fax?'

Whitney frowned.

'Yes, in the shop. Why?'

'Give me the number and check it in the morning.'

She hesitated, intrigued, and then told him. What harm could it do?

'I'll call you,' he promised and hung up.

He didn't know she lived above the shop and the fax was only twenty steps away. She raced down and waited impatiently for the machine to hum into life. It arrived within five minutes. Whitney tore the paper from the machine and raced back upstairs. Tucked up on the plump sofa in front of the television with a mug of coffee and two chocolate biscuits, she eagerly scanned the information.

As she started reading, she realised it was Zach's résumé, and grinned. He was thirty, two years her senior. His address was a smart apartment building in St Kilda Road. He'd graduated from the university of Melbourne, studied business, accounting, law and economics. A qualified pilot, too. Impressive but daunting. Their lives were miles apart.

She sighed and slid lower on the sofa. Should she take a gamble? Didn't Zach deserve at least one date for his persistence, and all those flowers?

She itched to satisfy her curiosity about the surprising instant awareness thing between them. Fate, Maz had said. Maybe it was. But she'd never know if she didn't take the chance, right? By the time she went to bed, she had changed her mind a dozen times.

Next day, Tess arrived at work looking no brighter than the day before. When Zach didn't call during the morning, Whitney felt keenly disappointed, forced to admit that he had only been flirting. Then around midday, she answered the phone with her usual, 'Good morning, Bygone Books.'

'Sorry. I had meetings all morning. Get my fax?'

Whitney's heart melted at the sound of his voice. She turned to see if Tess was paying attention. She was, great. All she needed was an audience.

'Yes.'

'So, what do you say?'

'You've been a busy man.'

'I meant going out with me.'

Now the moment of decision had arrived, Whitney hesitated. Last night she had almost decided to agree but in the cold light of day, she wavered.

'Probably not a good idea.'

'More questions?'

'A thousand, and twice as many doubts.'

'Then don't think. Go with your instincts.'

'I don't think so.'

Eavesdropping, Tess gasped and gestured wildly. Whitney scowled and waved her away.

'Why not?' he was persisting.

'Why?' she countered.

'We're attracted. Let's explore it.'

Was he kidding? All kinds of warm and wonderful feelings flowed through her when she heard his voice and thought about him, which had been every waking moment and half the night. She felt like an obsessed schoolgirl with a crush, not pushing thirty.

'I doubt we have much in common.'

'Then let's take each other as we are and find out. Take a chance, Whitney,' he urged softly.

She caught her breath. She wasn't big on risks. Plot and plan was her motto. But he was saying all the right things.

'Lunch is a perfect opportunity to get acquainted. It's all organised.'

'What is?' she asked, intrigued.

'Our picnic.'

Amused, Whitney looked out the window at the steady rain that had been soaking Melbourne all week.

'Does your office have a window?' she asked.

'Sure.'

'Then you'll have noticed the weather. Where can we picnic in this rain?'

'Woman, have a little faith,' he drawled.

Whitney imagined the grin on his face at the other end. She glanced at the shop wall clock about to strike twelve.

'I only have an hour.'

'I'll have you back in sixty minutes,' his instant reply came.

'I don't see how.'

'Trust me,' he coaxed. 'Everything's under control. Can you be ready in five minutes?'

Whitney panicked and dithered with

excitement. Maybe it wouldn't hurt. Maybe for once in her life she should take a chance, have a little fun.

'All right,' she conceded. 'I'll go out with you, but just this once,' she added quickly.

As she hung up, she caught Tess grinning.

'Don't you dare breathe a word of this to Maz,' Whitney threatened.

'It's so romantic,' Tess sighed.

Whitney moaned.

'It's crazy and I just know I'm going to regret it.'

2

Depending on the circumstances, five minutes can fly or it can drag. For Whitney, it flew. Upstairs in her flat, she considered changing from her comfortable work clothes but didn't have time. Besides, Zach would know she had fussed and she didn't want him to know how desperately she longed to make a good impression.

Instinct made Whitney glance down on to the wet street to see a black limousine sweep into the kerb. When Zach emerged, she sighed with anticipation. She grabbed her bag and her raincoat from its peg, since it was obvious they were going to get drenched, and started downstairs.

On the landing, she slowed and sauntered to the bottom as though she had all the time in the world. Zach's brilliant smile made her feel as special as Cinderella and all of her inhibitions slid away. As she descended, he stepped forward to the bottom of the stairs and held out his hand. She curled her fingers into his. The contact sent a thrill racing through her body.

'Be back in an hour, Tess. Right?'

'Absolutely.'

He winked at Tess and she giggled.

As they dashed across the pavement in the rain, a waiting, uniformed chauffeur opened the limousine door. Zach climbed in and pulled Whitney after him. Laughing and brushing off raindrops, Whitney sank into the deep comfort of plush beige upholstery and tried not to appear too impressed.

This was the first time she had ever been completely alone with Zach. Whitney waited for the chauffeur to get in and drive them off, but nothing happened. Instead, he opened an umbrella and walked away down the street. Whitney turned to Zach.

'Where's he going?'

'Not far. I hope you like chicken and champagne.'

He pressed a button and a bottle of champagne nestling on ice slid out from behind a concealed, polished-timber panel. He filled two crystal flutes. Whitney suddenly caught on.

'We're staying here, in front of the shop at a parking meter?'

He smiled and handed her a glass.

'Cheers.'

Amused, Whitney shook her head and sipped the bubbly wine. Behind tinted windows, ensconced in sumptuous privacy, she felt completely indulged. Like big, gentle arms, the soft, leather seats wrapped around her, seducing her to snuggle into their comfort and enjoy. Zach flicked a switch on a console that looked as complicated as an aeroplane flight deck and stereo music softly drifted around them. Another door opened to reveal a platter of chicken salad and caviar savouries.

'Hungry?' he inquired.

A sparkle lightened his soft grey eyes. She accepted a drumstick.

'This fantastic limousine is yours?' she inquired.

Zach shook his head.

'Heavens, no. It's showy and unnecessary. It belongs to my father. He dusts it off for special occasions.'

'He let you borrow it?'

'Theoretically. My parents are overseas. The perfect solution to our damp dilemma, wouldn't you agree? What about your folks?'

Zach wasn't eating much, just watching her and drinking.

'Working people,' she replied, voicing the fact which only emphasised the difference between them. 'My mother has been with Caringfords for over twenty years. I go there sometimes to window-shop and dream.'

Zach raised his eyebrows.

'It's the store to buy jewellery. That where you bought your necklace?'

Whitney smiled fondly and fingered the circle of black opal, flashing dark blue lights and fire, set in the filigree cradle of a golden heart.

'No. It was a gift from my father. He's an opal miner in Coober Pedy.'

Zach tilted his head to one side.

'Your parents are divorced?'

Whitney shook her head.

'They never bothered. Separated.'

He didn't pursue the issue and she was grateful.

'Brothers and sisters?'

'None.'

She glanced down at her hands but, with a gentle touch beneath her chin, Zach lifted her gaze to meet his.

'What about you?'

She gave a small, self-conscious laugh. Their gazes met and she held her breath. He couldn't possibly feel as attracted as she did, could he?

'What you see is what you get,' she replied impishly.

'That's why I asked you out.'

She was drawn into the smoky depths of his eyes again, fascinated and hypnotised. He looked so handsome and sincere. Strands of soft dark hair fell over his forehead. Whitney just knew if she touched them, the fine wisps would be as light as silk.

'Well?' he probed.

'Well, what?'

'You.'

'What about me?'

'Where did you grow up?'

Finished eating, she wiped her hands on the crisp white napkin Zach had spread across her knee, cringing as she soiled it.

'Here in Melbourne, with my mother, then joined my father in school holidays, except summer. Mother claimed it was too hot in the outback but I always rather suspected her motives were more selfish. I loved being with him and I think she was afraid I might want to go and live with him.'

'Did you?'

'Not really. The outback is different and interesting but isolated. You need to be a special person to live out there.'

'Why did they separate?'

'Mother hated the outback and Father wouldn't leave it. You either love it or you don't.'

'Do you?'

'I did back then. I couldn't wait for the holidays. But since leaving school and working, I can only get out to visit maybe once a year. My father never comes to the city.'

'I've flown over much of the outback,' Zach said, and Whitney remembered he was a pilot. 'It's a stark and beautiful place but, as you say, only a certain breed of person can live out there.'

'Mm, and the colours. They start soft in the morning and sharpen. And that intense blue sky . . . '

As her thoughts drifted, Whitney settled deeper into her seat, feeling mellow, eating the strawberries Zach offered from a silver dish. They were chilled and delicious.

Zach poured the last of the champagne into their glasses. Whitney blinked. Had they drunk the whole bottle? Her mind wouldn't function for the rest of the day! Until the effects of the alcohol wore off, she couldn't tell if this heady happiness was from the wine or Zach's company.

'I usually take holidays and visit Dad in winter,' Whitney continued. 'But I couldn't get away this year. Dad's not much of a letter writer but we keep in touch regularly. What about your family?'

He drained the last of his champagne and set down the glass.

'My father's in property development.'

Recognition clicked over in Whitney's mind and she gaped.

'Your father is one half of Chandler and Forman?'

Zach shrugged and silently assessed her with his calm grey gaze.

'They own half of Australia,' she whispered.

Zach threw back his head and laughed.

'A good chunk of it anyway.'

'You didn't join him in the business?'

Zach eyed her shrewdly.

'I wanted to control my own life.'

'Ah. I see.'

'And my mother,' he said with a

twisted smile, 'has a heavy, social calendar. She works hard for charity. I have two married sisters, two brothers-in-law and six nieces and nephews.'

He deliberately omitted Melanie, who had proved selfish and shallow. She had been relegated to his past. A successful and intuitive stockbroker, he prided himself on his good judgement, but Melanie was the worst mistake he had ever made.

It hadn't taken Zach long to realise that the social-climbing Melanie paled in comparison to someone like Whitney Leighton. To his amazement, Melanie had even hinted at marriage but their disagreements and incompatibilities warned him. Two weeks ago she had stormed out and he hadn't seen her since, nor did he have any intention of pursuing her with a view to reconciliation. They would both be wasting their time. They simply weren't meant for each other.

When his concentration refocused, Zach caught Whitney staring. Pulled by the unexplained magic between them and his intense gaze, she found herself leaning closer. Then, from the corner of her eye, she glimpsed the chauffeur outside the window. Zach followed her gaze, groaned and kissed her cheek, whispering, 'Time's up,' with a sigh.

Whitney stifled her disappointment at the interruption but enjoyed the touch of his lips on her face. Their picnic had been wonderful. She gathered her wits and her unused raincoat, knowing the interlude had been a surreal escape, but reality beckoned. She alighted from the sleek vehicle and, as she moved away, Zach's big warm hand curled firmly around her wrist.

'I'll call,' he said as the car pulled away from the kerb.

Dreamily, she returned to the shop — and the excited Tess!

'You can't see a thing through those dark tinted limousine windows,' Tess grumbled.

'That's the idea. Been busy?'

Tess shook her head, reached for a

tissue and sneezed. Whitney was swamped with a rush of pity.

'Tess, go home and stay there until you're completely better.'

'But we have all that indexing to do.'

'Don't worry about a thing. It's my responsibility. If I get busy, I'll call Susan, OK?'

'Are you sure?'

Whitney gathered up Tess's bag and propelled her to the door.

'Yes. Now go.'

Looking miserable but grateful, Tess left. Whitney sighed as the jingling of the doorbell gradually faded and she watched the girl scurry for a tram. She had a pile of work. Without Tess, it was just going to take longer.

Between customers, working on the computer and shelving books, Whitney's thoughts constantly returned like a boomerang to Zach. Resembling a whirlwind sweeping in with the spring rain the day before, Whitney knew a powerful force had entered her life and suspected it would never be the same again. She didn't dare contemplate where it would lead, or end.

Frowning, her thoughts reverted to the shop dilemma. Last week, it had been her life. Now it seemed likely all her efforts in building the business would be for someone else's benefit. When she found time, she would telephone the banks but, without any assets for collateral, she knew any possibility of a loan was remote.

Adding to her workload, a new shipment of books arrived. Whitney surveyed the crates. Mrs Pearce's middle-aged bachelor son, Edward, had been busy, as always. It was exciting discovering what treasures he found on his countryside ramblings. Old and rare books of Australiana were keenly collected. The precious acquisitions would need to be carefully handled, sorted and catalogued into the computer, which meant working late every night and probably all weekend until it was done.

As if in telepathic thought, the florist,

with whom Whitney was now on first-name terms, delivered a single ivory rose. There was no card but it was unnecessary and the gesture lifted Whitney's spirits. She closed her eyes and inhaled deeply the bloom's musky fragrance, caressing its velvet petals. Then she set it in a slender vase on the counter to remind her of the sender.

That night, while Maz went to the movies with Hugo, her muscled aerobics instructor, Whitney topped up the water in all the vases throughout the flat, and then went downstairs to open the first of the book crates. She had hardly begun when the telephone rang.

'Too soon to ask you out again?'

Whitney smiled at the sound of his voice and cast a despairing glance at the crates.

'Whatever you have in mind, I'm afraid the answer's no.'

'I thought you enjoyed our lunch,' he said, sounding genuinely disappointed.

'Don't sulk,' Whitney teased. 'You know I did.'

As she talked, she retrieved a rare book of original, colonial sketches in excellent condition. Oh, my, she thought, sitting on the floor and opening the book with almost religious reverence. Zach's brother-in-law would love this.

'I'm swamped with work at the moment. Tess is off sick indefinitely and I have a mountain of indexing.'

After a moment's pause, Zach said, 'Well, take care,' and hung up.

Puzzled by his unusual abruptness, Whitney frowned. Admittedly, she barely knew him but his reaction seemed out of character. She hated refusing Zach but, in the light of her workload at the moment, she simply had no choice. And this time, she realised, he hadn't promised to call again.

3

Next day, the spring weather improved. The weak sun was accompanied by a fresh wind but at least the rain had cleared and business was brisk. Whitney's morning in the shop was hectic without Tess and she despaired of getting a break.

Then, as if on cue, Zach arrived. Whitney's heart lifted at the unexpected and refreshing sight of him. His hair drifted back off his face in controlled style and his eyes glinted across at her with warmth.

'What do you have there?' she asked as she eyed the plastic bag he placed on the counter.

Its contents wafted a spicy aroma.

'Asian takeaway.'

He removed a carton and waved it tantalisingly under her nose.

'I'll trade it for a kiss.'

Whitney darted her gaze around the shop and its browsing customers.

'I can't,' she whispered.

'No such word.'

She whisked another glance over her shoulder, leaned across the counter and gave him a quick kiss. Zach sighed and reluctantly handed over the meal.

'You're a hard woman.'

But surely he knew he could melt her with a touch or a glance? She transferred her attention to the food and inhaled deeply. Zach moved around behind the counter.

'You go and eat. I'll watch the shop.'

'You know about books?'

'I can learn.'

'Who's running your business while you're running mine?'

'Samantha, my personal assistant.'

Samantha — sounded like a gorgeous, leggy blonde. Whitney discovered herself stung by a flash of jealousy.

'Lunch hour can be busy,' she pointed out.

'I'll ask for help if I need to.'

Helpless and delighted, she agreed and retired to the tiny office-cum-storeroom at the back of the shop.

Possessed with the art of easy conversation, Zach charmed all customers with practised finesse and dealt with all problems easily.

'Want these moved somewhere before I leave?' he asked when Whitney rejoined him after lunch, indicating the boxes behind the counter.

'No, thanks. I'll need to work on them here tonight.'

'More overtime?' he accused softly.

'Afraid so.'

'I'll come and help.'

Amazed by his offer, she was about to protest when he placed a finger gently against her lips.

'No argument. I'll bring dinner. Seven.'

He kissed her on the nose and winked. Dumbfounded, she nodded. When was he getting his work done?

After he left, Whitney expelled a long

sigh, wondering how wise she was to continue their friendship. So far, it was all too good to be true. She knew little about Zach's life except that he was well-bred and cultured, and she found the knowledge intimidating.

That evening, Whitney was rummaging in crates when Zach tapped on the shop window carrying a huge, cardboard box. She unlocked the door and let him in. His old jeans and black polo shirt were endearing contrasts to his usual business suits, the casual clothes making him more appealing and approachable, more on her level. She cringed at her thoughts. Zach was always open and normal with her, generous with his time and attention, treating her as an equal. There was no reason for the deep sense of inadequacy she suffered.

'I hope that's not full of food,' she teased, pushing her wayward thoughts aside as he set the box on the counter.

'You look good enough to eat,' he murmured.

When he pulled her playfully against him, he smelled of a woodsy fragrance. She rested her hands against his chest.

'Maybe we should eat,' she suggested, her heart pounding.

'Maybe you should thank me for buying dinner.'

His humour and playful mood were infectious and she couldn't resist a kiss. It was so good, they repeated it, the second one lasting much longer. Afterwards, they stood locked together, emotions absorbed, both overwhelmed by its impact.

Whitney's thoughts unscrambled enough to realise that Zach had burrowed his way into her heart. In three days, this man monopolised her life and filled her thoughts, a man who had the potential to become very important in her life. As they moved apart, Zach eased over the moment by delving into the box he had brought. He spread a tablecloth over one of the book crates, set two candlesticks on either side and, with an exaggerated flourish, placed a white paper parcel in the centre. Whitney beamed.

'Fish and chips by candlelight. Marvellous.'

He snapped open two cans of soft drinks.

'Cheers.'

Whitney giggled.

'I would have thought the only fish you'd eat was caviar.'

'Not on Wednesdays.'

His sensational smile almost toppled Whitney off her feet.

'Here's to old books and fast food,' she quipped.

Zach perched on the corner of an empty crate and Whitney sat on her office chair as they licked their salty fingers, shared their day, and laughed.

'I'll do the dishes,' Zach offered when they finished, rolling up the paper and tossing it into the wastebin like a basketball shot.

'Let's get down to work.'

He rubbed his hands together with enthusiasm.

'What's first?'

Hand on hips, Whitney stood back.

'Open the rest of these boxes.'

As he set about the task, Whitney watched him eagerly, awaiting the first books to be removed.

'I never know how rare they might be.'

'When is a book judged antiquarian?' Zach asked as he removed the first ones.

'If it's over one hundred years old.'

He quietly whistled.

'What makes them valuable?'

'Subject matter or content mostly, or it might be a first edition or extremely rare and the price range is virtually open-ended. And condition is always important. Then of course they need to be complete. If any leaves are missing the value is reduced. Our buyer, Edward, is meticulous when it comes to selection.'

'Sounds like I should be investing in some of these as well as shares,' Zach quipped.

'Wouldn't hurt.' Whitney shrugged

and smiled. 'The prices of blue-chip books can double every few years. They're a steady investment.'

When all the crates were empty, Zach carted the packaging to the recycling bin at the back of the shop. Meanwhile, Whitney had been sorting them according to subject so that now she turned on the computer and began keying in details.

'How did you become interested in books?' Zach asked when he returned, sitting on the shop counter browsing through a volume.

'My father collected all kinds of books on his travels around Australia when he was younger,' Whitney replied, looking up from the computer as she spoke. 'In school holidays, I read everything from National Geographic to science fiction to classics. I acquired an appreciation for them all.'

She smiled with nostalgia.

'When I was small, he read to me at night or told me wonderful stories about how he came by each book.

Other times, I'd settle into a corner and read while he sat around with his mates playing cards, drinking and gambling.'

'What's he like?'

A soft, indulgent smile edged across her face.

'A big, quiet man. We looked after each other. I think you'd like him.'

She blushed at revealing the personal sentiment.

Hours later, still only half finished and exhausted, Whitney yawned and stretched. She rubbed her neck and glanced across at Zach, engrossed in reading. Smiling, she watched him for a moment. He looked up and caught her stare. Embarrassed and guilty, she looked away and shut down the computer.

'That's enough for tonight. Thanks for your help. I can manage the rest of these over the next few days.'

'Oh, no, you don't!'

He confined her in the chair by placing his hands either side of its arms.

'What do you mean?'

'I'll help until we've finished. Otherwise I won't get to see you again.'

He drew her off the chair and pulled her against him.

'I'll take you home.'

'Actually, I live quite close.'

'Really?'

He nibbled her ear, then their lips met.

Suddenly, a familiar voice said, 'Hi, I'm Maz. You must be Zach.'

Startled by the interruption, they broke apart. Whitney glared at her flatmate, wearing green and orange floral leggings, a purple baggy jumper and an impish grin. Zach extended a hand towards her.

'I am. Nice to meet you.'

'Enjoy the movie?' Whitney asked with cool reserve.

Maz screwed up her nose.

'Just thought I'd come down and see how you were doing.'

'We're doing fine.'

'So I see.'

Whitney sensed Zach shaking with

concealed laughter beside her.

'Well, I'll see you soon.'

Maz turned a pair of innocent, sparkling eyes over them before darting back upstairs.

'Oh, you can count on that,' Whitney called after her with a tight smile. Zach grinned in amusement.

'You have to stop seducing men in public places, Whitney,' he murmured.

She gasped, speechless.

'What does Maz stand for?' he asked.

'Maria Zarelli. And boy is she going to get it,' Whitney muttered.

'How on earth did she get in here? The front door's locked.'

'Fire escape outside.'

'Who is she?'

'My flatmate.'

'Where did she go?'

'Upstairs.'

Whitney could see Zach's mind slotting all the information together.

'You live above the shop?'

She nodded. He looked fascinated but not judgmental.

'Handy.'

Whitney shrugged.

'Rent's cheap. Sorry about Maz. She's the loveliest friend but she has absolutely no tact.'

'No problem. It was rather enjoyable until she interrupted.'

He slid an arm around her waist.

'See you tomorrow night.'

In a haze of joy that he shared her pleasure, Whitney frowned in confusion, thinking she must have missed something.

'I'm sorry?'

'Here. Let's see if we can't finish what we started.'

His ambiguous words were intriguing but told her that at least she'd see him again. She shouldn't. He must have other things to do, people in his life, friends, obligations. Whitney felt confused, torn by emotions pulling her in one direction and commonsense in another.

Truthfully, she felt overwhelmed by her life at the moment — a new relationship; the extra workload; the imminent shop sale dilemma and frustrating hopelessness of trying to raise the deposit money fast. Then she looked at Zach and knew she wouldn't trade their chance meeting for the world. All her other troubles faded into insignificance.

As if reading the ocean of words on her mind, Zach planted a firm, departing kiss on her mouth and flashed a warm, encouraging smile as he left. Then, with a last check around the shop and stifling a yawn, Whitney turned out the lights and went upstairs.

'Don't forget I have a party at Hugo's tonight,' Maz reminded her the following morning.

'I'll be working late.'

'Alone?'

'No.'

'All right! This guy, Zach, is a mega babe.'

'He's just helping me with indexing.'

'More like helping himself,' Maz said with a chuckle.

'It was just a kiss!' Whitney protested.

Zach returned that night and continued helping Whitney. With his intense concentration and her fast keyboarding skills, they eventually finished just before midnight. Relieved, Whitney rose from her chair and stretched.

'Thank you, Zach. I appreciate all you've done.'

'My pleasure.'

'Now you can get your own life back.'

'I don't believe I really had one until I met you. I love being with you.'

Whitney glowed beneath his intense, warm gaze.

'Me, too,' she murmured, elevating their relationship to the next level. 'Coffee?' she offered uncertainly.

'Love some.'

She led him through the back of the shop and upstairs.

'How's Tess?'

Whitney was pleased he remembered to ask and it doubled her respect for him.

'Miserable. Seems she has a nasty

dose of the flu. I phoned her mother this morning. She'll be off all week.'

She paused in the kitchenette and indicated the adjoining, small sitting room.

'Make yourself comfortable. I'll boil the kettle.'

When it was ready, she took in a tray and set it on the low table. Zach lounged on the sofa, dwarfing its size, watching the television news.

'Seems you have an admirer.'

He glanced at the flowers. They shared a smile. His perceptive gaze swept the cosy room.

'This is homely. I like it.'

A wave of relief washed through her. His comment instantly set her at ease but she knew him well enough by now to realise he meant it. His city apartment would be much more luxurious.

'How do you take it?' she asked and indicated his mug.

'Black. Straight up.'

He patted the sofa beside him.

'Come here.'

A comfortable silence fell between them while they listened to the weather report and the late movie was announced.

'One of my favourites,' Whitney said.

'Mind if I stay and watch it with you?'

'No, of course not.'

Snuggled against him, Whitney relaxed, but the busy week took its toll and her eyelids soon grew heavy. Desperately, she fought them but Zach's shoulder was so big and comfortable. She closed her eyes for just a moment, intending to listen to the movie without watching it.

The next thing she knew was the gentle brush of lips on her face. When her eyes fluttered open, Whitney's gaze settled on the small mantel clock. It was early morning and the movie credits were scrolling! She had fallen sleep for over an hour! Embarrassed, she sat up.

'Why didn't you wake me?' she asked in a sleepy voice.

He shrugged.

'Selfish, I guess. You looked so

47

beautiful. I've been thinking. You've been working too hard lately. You deserve a night out. How about dinner tomorrow night? No takeaways, I promise.'

Whitney had planned to phone her mother about the dreaded subject of money and a possible loan. Then she thought, what the heck? If she forgot about the problem, maybe it would go away. And she knew where she would rather be.

'I guess I could be persuaded.'

They kissed with deep warmth and a flare of passion.

'Did that work?'

His voice was husky.

'Mr Chandler, you've got a date.'

4

A continuous noise penetrated Whitney's dream, drawing her into consciousness. As she emerged from sleep, she realised it was the telephone. She opened one eye, checked the clock and groaned. She never overslept! She reached out and grabbed the receiver.

'Good morning. Did I wake you?'

'Actually, yes.'

Whitney couldn't hide her grumpiness even though it was Zach.

'Are you still in bed?'

Whitney sighed and clutched the quilt around her.

'Yes, but not for long.'

'So am I.'

Whitney blinked aside an evocative vision of him, appalled by her intimate thoughts. Reluctantly, she rolled out of bed and padded barefoot with the cordless phone across to her wardrobe as she talked.

'Then you're late, too,' she quipped.

'Don't forget dinner tonight.'

'Unlikely.'

'Where are we going?'

'You'll find out.'

Whitney frowned at the clock.

'I'm sorry, Zach, I only have thirty minutes to shower, dress, eat and open the shop.'

'Are you trying to get rid of me?'

'Yes.'

She laughed and hung up.

For the first time ever, she was late and ran downstairs to find early customers waiting patiently outside. After that, the day grew steadily worse. Normally, she thrived on busy days, extending herself for customers. Instead, she fought panic. With Zach being mysterious about where they would dine, she was terrified of disappointing him and worried about it all day. By six, after waiting for a tedious browser, resulting in a large sale, she practically pushed him out of the door and sped upstairs. Having showered, she then stood barefoot in the centre of her bedroom in her best black satin and lace chemise, and moaned.

'I look so . . . unglamorous.'

'We're not finished yet,' Maz bubbled with reassurance.

'But my hair.'

Whitney fussed, piling it on her head. She freed a few wisps for effect then let it wing down again.

'I don't know what to do with it.'

'Definitely down,' Maz told her. 'Men love long, tousled hair. It's sexy.' Maz removed a black dress from its hanger.

'Put this on.'

'I hardly have a choice,' Whitney said wryly.

She slipped it on and cast a despairing eye over herself in the mirror.

'It's not good enough.'

Maz scoffed and waved a hand.

'It's perfect. Long enough to be

decent and short enough to be cheeky. And with your long legs,' she uttered an envious sigh, 'he'll love it.'

Unconvinced but lacking another option, Whitney added a thick gold chain and matching bracelet, a twenty-first birthday present from her mother. She spread on a thick gloss of burgundy lipstick and pulled back one side of her hair in a stylish sweep with a black and gold comb.

'Now, turn around,' Maz instructed. 'Slowly.'

She cast a critical eye over her friend.

'Well, if he doesn't like the package, it won't be because of the wrapping.'

When Zach arrived fifteen minutes later, his slow gaze roamed over Whitney with deep appreciation. He looked dangerously handsome himself in a dark grey suit, round-collared shirt and no tie. Whitney breathed a silent sigh of relief. She was appropriately dressed after all.

'You're looking particularly gorgeous tonight, Miss Leighton.'

He kissed her nose. As they walked downstairs arm in arm, her fitted dress strained against her every curve. The idling limousine gleamed beneath the fairy lights that twinkled in the trees along Collins Street. With familiar ease, she slid into the back seat. This time the vehicle did move off and they headed out on to the freeway. Quiet expectation hummed between them as they drove and there was little need for conversation. Whitney didn't fully concentrate on their destination until the vehicle whispered to a halt at the airport, alongside a small, executive jet.

'We're eating in that?' she exclaimed.

Zach chuckled.

'You seemed to enjoy the fish and chips so much the other night, I thought you might appreciate a favourite and discreet little seafood restaurant I know on Sydney harbour.'

Feeling guilty for misgivings, Whitney wondered if discreet meant sheltered from public gaze or merely private.

'Interstate just for dinner?'

Then realisation dawned and she remembered he was a pilot. Reading her thoughts, Zach took her hand and led her up the steps and on board.

'I won't be at the controls tonight. I promise you my undivided attention.'

As they buckled their seat belts, he glanced across at her and she smiled. Whitney Leighton was the loveliest, most natural woman he'd ever met but too uncertain of herself, without cause. From his first sight of her on the stepladder, he had been hit with a strong attraction, a deep chemistry he had never felt with any other woman. Already, he knew they were right for each other but Whitney would take some convincing.

The flight was smooth, filled with easy conversation and a crisp, refreshing white wine. Within an hour, they had landed in Sydney and another limousine whisked them into the city. The restaurant on the North Shore was exclusive and intimate, richly carpeted and softly lit. Situated directly on the

54

waterfront with a wall of panoramic windows, the view across the water to the city was breathtaking.

'Good evening, Mr Chandler,' the head waiter greeted Zach. 'Your table is ready.'

Once settled into the plush, semi-circular, private dining alcove, he ordered wine and oysters. The atmosphere was intimate and romantic, and Whitney barely contained the emotional disturbance racing through her body. Zach caught her hand and squeezed it.

'Relax,' he whispered, leaning close.

Whitney returned an apprehensive smile. She was in special company, in a special place and she was crazy not to be savouring the experience. Who knew how long this magic would last? Their friendship was still so new and fragile, the future unknown.

When the waiter served entrée, Whitney gasped. A string of pearls lay draped among her oysters on ice! This was too much. Flattered but distressed, she met Zach's gaze to soften her refusal.

'I can't accept them.'

'Of course you can,' he said, lightly dismissing her concern.

Whitney placed a trembling hand over the cool, milky gems.

'They're superb but . . . '

'Extravagant?'

'Zach, this is incredibly thoughtful, and everything an awestruck, working girl could want, but I simply can't. It's too generous.'

He grew serious and sought her hands, enfolding them within his own.

'Don't take away my pleasure. They're not to buy you,' he murmured, addressing the question in her eyes. 'They're an expression of my feelings for you.'

How could she not trust the sincerity in his voice and genuine warmth in his gaze, and refuse? Feeling as though she betrayed her conscience, Whitney surrendered.

'Only because you insist. I'll treasure them.'

56

Between entrée and main course, they danced. When Zach took her in his arms, Whitney felt like she'd come home. This was where she belonged. Their attraction had deepened with such alarming speed, it left her breathless. Zach pulled her tighter and rested his chin against her forehead.

Despite their different social backgrounds, Whitney was falling in love and was frightened of her overwhelming emotions. She decided to trust her instinct and live for the moment and the completeness she felt with this man, not daring to consider that it might not last.

Their seafood was delicious and exquisitely presented. The dinner, the restaurant, the flight from Melbourne was all so indulgent and lavish. It was so ironic that Zach had so much money and she was so desperately in need of it. Compared to this evening and Zach, her budget-ridden life was mundane, but the reality engendered only respect for him and his achievements, not envy.

After a decadent chocolate dessert and coffee, Zach enticed her on to the floor for more dancing. Combined with a busy week and late night, Whitney grew languid and stifled a yawn. Zach frowned with concern.

'You're exhausted.'

'I'm sorry. It's been a fabulous evening.'

'But we should leave. Time to get you home, Sleeping Beauty.'

In the limousine, somewhere between the restaurant and the airport, Whitney fell asleep. Without Zach's support, she would never have made it on to the plane and only woke as it touched down again in Melbourne.

'Am I so boring?' Zach teased gently as they sped along the freeway.

'Never.'

She snuggled closer against him and they kissed.

'I'd like to take you home to Winsmere on Sunday night, for dinner,' he murmured.

'Your parents are back?'

The news stirred Whitney to wakefulness and attention. Zach nodded.

'What's the matter?' he asked, noticing her scowl.

'Is it necessary?'

'It is to me.'

'They'll hardly approve.'

'They're not dating you. I am. Any objections are only in your mind.'

Whitney couldn't argue with such logic. She felt inadequate yet Zach always made her feel special, important even, and spoiled. His feelings for her went far beyond money. Helping her out in the shop this week had proven that. So she suppressed her reservations.

'All right.'

After Zach kissed her goodnight, Whitney crept upstairs and tiptoed through the flat, wondering how on earth she would afford another outfit for the family dinner. She sank into bed and succumbed to an uneasy sleep.

In the morning, to her surprise and relief, Tess returned to work. She was promptly left in charge while Whitney headed for the department stores. It took hours and aching feet before she found the perfect dress, cringed as she paid for it on credit card and carried it home.

Never speechless, Maz gasped as Whitney dressed on Sunday night for the Chandler dinner. The ivory satin gown clung to her like another skin and its trembling sheen trapped the light with a creamy glow. Whitney had decided on simplicity and elegance to which she added Zach's pearls.

'Dinner with the folks means you're up for appraisal,' Maz said.

'I know,' Whitney groaned. 'I hope I pass.'

'Opposites can work.'

'But do they last? Socially, we're completely mismatched.'

'Does it bother him?'

'It doesn't seem to,' Whitney admitted, 'but call me pessimistic. I can't help sensing we're a disaster just waiting to happen.'

When Zach arrived a short time later, he pulled Whitney against him.

'You look like a goddess,' he said so tenderly.

Downstairs, the limousine once more graced the kerb. They moved off along Collins Street, then crossed the Yarra River and headed south from the city. They drove through exclusive, leafy streets, past substantial, luxurious homes until they turned into a pillared driveway.

As they entered the high-fenced property, the headlights glinted off a brass nameplate and the vehicle whispered around the semi-circular driveway before drawing to a stop in front of a floodlit, Georgian mansion.

Whitney gasped as Zach quietly said, 'Welcome to Winsmere.'

5

Whitney's eyes were transfixed on the magnificent building. She shivered involuntarily and turned to Zach in panic.

'Turn the car around. Take me home.'

Zach glanced at her, frowning with concern.

'Whitney,' he whispered with such sensitivity she almost stopped breathing, 'trust me. You're perfect.'

He placed a reassuring hand over hers.

'You're wonderful for morale,' she whispered back.

'You wore the pearls,' he observed.

'I thought they'd add some class,' she answered quietly.

'Is that what this is all about? You're feeling daunted?'

'Wouldn't you?'

'Probably, but there's no need. I take people as I find them. And, I'm glad I found you. So stop worrying.'

The instant Whitney set foot inside Winsmere, even with Zach's supporting hand at her waist, she repressed awe and panic to summon every grain of courage she possessed, sensing she was going to need it. More like a palace than a home, the grand residence quietly screamed wealth. Whitney scanned the marbled entry hall, the chandelier, the sweeping staircase beyond. Antiques stood everywhere, and so much space. Her entire flat would easily fit into one corner of this area alone.

Then, as if from nowhere, the Chandlers appeared to join them. Zach and his parents exchanged formal greetings.

'Zachary, dear.'

His mother turned a cheek for his kiss, her gaze darting over her son's shoulder for a covert glimpse of his companion, but it was his father to whom Whitney was first introduced.

She waited for release from his excruciating handshake. Everton Chandler, with distinguished grey wavy hair and a moustache, looked older than she expected and his piercing gaze judged her unkindly before she had barely spoken her greeting. In the absence of a welcoming smile, she realised she had been catalogued and filed away as insignificant, dismissed as unimportant with a single glance.

Deeply crushed because of the expense and effort she had made to appear acceptable, Whitney was made clearly aware, at least in her host's estimation, of her failure. Unlike her husband, Muriel Chandler had aged well. The petite, thin woman wore an exquisite emerald and diamond necklace, highlighting an elegantly-understated designer gown of the same colour. Her ash-blonde hair was stylishly upswept and subtly tinted.

'I'm pleased to meet you.'

Whitney suffered a twinge of guilt for uttering words she did not mean and concealed her hurt behind a forced smile.

'Muriel, please,' Zach's mother replied. The polite request was shallow and insincere.

'Zachary, have you seen Melanie lately?' Muriel asked with transparent innocence, possessively clutching his arm as they crossed the hall.

'As I've already told you, Mother, we don't see each other anymore,' he replied, unsmiling.

'Ah, of course.'

Muriel's insipid smile betrayed the true reason she had raised the subject.

'Our families are old friends,' she addressed Whitney in explanation. 'Zach and Melanie grew up together. They're extremely close.'

'Were, mother,' Zach replied firmly.

The party entered a burgundy sitting-room, rich with velvet drapes, deep carpet and soft, leather chairs. A gilt-framed mirror glinted from its place above a marble fireplace, a small but warming fire in the grate. It added a welcoming atmosphere their hosts failed to provide. The façade continued while they sipped cocktails and made polite conversation about the city, the weather, Everton's gold and Muriel's garden.

After the longest thirty minutes Whitney had ever endured, a uniformed maid eventually announced dinner and they moved into the adjoining dining-room. A vast, polished table, large enough to seat twenty people, gleamed with cutlery and crystal in the soft glow from yet another magnificent chandelier. A servant seated them a mile apart and they peered across the table at each other over lavish bowls of pink rosebuds.

During the early part of dinner, Whitney concentrated on her line of silver cutlery, watched and observed. Had she been even tepidly welcomed, she might have participated more enthusiastically. Her occasional glance across the broad expanse of table at Zach caught his positive, mischievous grin. Obviously inured to such proceedings, his presence sustained her over the awkward situation. Apparently, Zach's invitation tonight was to discreetly and politely inform his parents of their friendship. Whitney could only dread the consequences.

'Zach hasn't told us anything about you, Whitney,' Everton boomed from his end of the table, drawing her unwillingly into the conversation.

She paused in her enjoyment of the portion of lamb and vegetables on the gold-rimmed white china plate.

'I work at Bygone Books in Collins Street.'

'You own it?' he asked hopefully.

Whitney repressed a smile.

'No. I'm the manager. We specialise in Australiana.'

'Our son-in-law, Walter, collects historical Australian works,' Muriel said.

'Zach ordered books for his birthday recently. That's how we met.'

Whitney could see Muriel turning over that juicy piece of information in her mind, convinced she would be classified as an ambitious salesgirl with an eye on the main chance.

'Do you have family in Melbourne?'

'Only my mother. She's been with Caringfords for twenty years.'

Everton raised his eyebrows in abrupt recognition.

'Laura Leighton is your mother?'

'Yes.'

Whitney sipped her wine, witness to the knowing glance he exchanged down the length of the table with his wife. Unquestionably, they would have patronised the exclusive store where her mother worked.

'And your father?' Everton barked.

'He's an opal miner in Coober Pedy.'

That little disclosure would definitely set her fate in concrete. To her credit and poise, although Muriel blanched with shock, she swiftly recovered.

'How fascinating,' she said insincerely. 'It must be extremely hard work.'

Whitney smiled fondly.

'It's a way of life. It's in his blood. Some of my best memories are of the holidays I spent with him in the outback.'

'How exciting for you,' Muriel said without enthusiasm.

To their credit, Whitney thought, no-one asked why her parents lived apart, and the words separation or divorce remained discreetly unvoiced. During dessert, talk centred on the city's prominent people. Well-known names were dropped like hailstones in a storm, and to her relief, Whitney was temporarily excluded from the conversation.

Later, over coffee in the burgundy sitting-room again, Muriel asked, 'Were you educated in Melbourne, Whitney?'

She nodded.

'I went directly from high school into the bookshop. I've been there ten years now.'

'Zachary distinguished himself at university,' Muriel shamelessly bragged. 'He has built a solid future in business. When he meets the right woman we expect him to produce a son and continue the family name.'

Too bad if it's a daughter, Whitney

thought grimly. In that moment, she just wanted to be alone with Zach, be overwhelmed by her feelings for him, a little pampered perhaps, if only for a while. If that was all he offered, she would accept it graciously without complaint and move on. Their brief interlude would become one of life's experiences upon which she would reflect and smile.

'They hated me!' Whitney groaned as they drove away from Winsmere.

Zach slid an arm around her.

'They're impossible to please.'

'They like Melanie,' she grumbled.

'Melanie isn't very nice,' he said softly.

'But you dated her.'

'For all the wrong reasons.'

'You shouldn't be dating me either. I'm not part of your parent's grand plan for the future.'

'Ah, but you're part of mine.'

He drew her into his arms and kissed her. Whitney closed her eyes, over-whelmed with pleasure. Presently, the limousine drew up in front of an apartment tower in St Kilda Road.

'Why are we stopping here?' Whitney asked, guessing why.

'This is where I live.'

'Which one's yours?'

'The penthouse. It has a great view, especially at night. Would you like to see it? Join me for a goodnight drink, then I'll see you get back to your flat, safe and sound, I promise!'

There was no pressure in his offer. It was an invitation she could accept or refuse as she chose.

'Yes, please,' she replied without hesitation, tossing caution to the wind. 'I've never seen a penthouse before.'

Whitney stood on the threshold of Zach's penthouse, her first impression one of subdued lighting and space. A wall of glass on the other side revealed a panoramic view of Melbourne by night. Drawn to it, she moved across the apartment.

'Do you like it?' Zach asked from behind her.

'What's not to like?' she breathed. 'It's fabulous.'

Zach opened the sliding door as the breathtaking sight beckoned them out across a wide, tiled balcony, green and lush with potted plants. In the crisp air, Whitney shivered and rubbed her arms. Zach removed his coat and draped it around her shoulders. When his arms slid around her and his mouth pressed against her hair, she could feel his heartbeat. Zach caught her hand and drew her back indoors.

'There's more.'

It was all luxurious and private and secure. The kitchen was a modern dream in black and white and chrome, and Zach's study a computerised communications centre. Still holding his hand, and quietly calm and expectant, Whitney trailed him up the wide, carpeted stairs to a mezzanine floor of bedrooms. At the front of the penthouse, the main suite revealed a similar glittering night view of the city and was furnished in royal blue and gold, looking masculine and deeply comfortable.

Zach caught her eye across the sweep of soft, luxuriant carpet between them and their gaze met. In that precious, suspended moment, Whitney realised how wholeheartedly she loved him.

Zach moved toward her, his honest gaze answering the hesitation in her eyes. Privately, she vowed not to think of tomorrow or the next day or the day after that. For whatever reason, they had been fated to meet. This moment was destined to be unforgettable, charged with commitment and passion. Without another second's hesitation, they closed the distance between them, hands reached out, bodies touched and they kissed.

'What if this doesn't work between us?' she whispered as they eventually pulled apart.

'Don't think. Just feel,' he urged. 'I'm not asking you to change. Just be you. I love Whitney Leighton exactly the way she is.'

'This is crazy. We've only known each other six days.'

'We can stop.'

She looked up at him and realised she had been blind and unrealistic in not admitting this wonderful, powerful love sooner.

'No,' she replied, shaking her head vigorously.

Since meeting Zach, she had swiftly and willingly lost her single identity, plunging helplessly into a commitment with no guarantees. It terrified her, but if she never took a chance, she might never know such happiness.

'I have something for you,' he whispered.

'Zach,' she protested, 'you know how I feel about gifts.'

'Ah, but this one's different. Close your eyes.'

Sensing it was pointless to argue, she did as she was told.

After a moment, he said, 'You can open them now.'

Her eyelids fluttered apart to see a

royal blue velvet box, a very small box. As Zach lifted the lid, Whitney gasped.

'To match your necklace,' he explained.

It was a large, single pearl cradled in a bed of diamonds on a gold band. Didn't Zach ever think small? Whitney loved it on sight but hesitated to touch it because it raised the question of exactly what it meant.

She soon found out.

'Whitney, I love you,' he said tenderly. 'Marry me.'

6

Zach's proposal was unexpected and Whitney was stunned. This past week had been the stuff of fantasies, beyond reality, a dream into which she had willingly been drawn. But their social differences and his parents' disapproval gnawed at her mind.

Whitney turned to face him, loosely in the circle of his arms. He looked adorably ruffled and vulnerable, those dreamy dove grey eyes lit with expectation, so she steeled herself against his appeal.

'I don't expect you to make an honest woman of me,' she hinted gently.

'What we have found together is special and you know it.'

Zach was right and that's what frightened her. They had fallen headlong in love, but marriage?

'I've never shared anything this fantastic with another woman,' Zach whispered into the silence. 'Not even close.'

'Don't tempt me,' she whispered.

'Why not?'

'I never thought . . . '

Zach waited. Unable to look into his eyes, Whitney rested her forehead against his chin.

'You're asking me to spend the rest of my life with you after knowing you for barely a week.'

'Don't you want to? I'm sure.'

'So am I,' she agreed fervently, clutching him tighter, 'but your family doesn't approve.'

He placed a finger beneath her chin and softly kissed her.

'We'll manage.'

Anxiously, Whitney shook her head.

'Your family is wealthy and stable. Mine is working-class and broken.'

'Your parents' marriage won't be our marriage,' Zach reminded her but his words couldn't remove her distress.

'You won't expect me to be a socialite wife, will you? I love my job.'

She didn't mention the possibility it mightn't be for much longer, but she would find another.

'Never.'

Zach had answered and dismissed each of her objections but, still filled with unease, Whitney remained cautious. He removed the ring from its satin nest, reached out and took Whitney's hand.

'We're on the threshold of something wonderful and I refuse to let it go.'

Still fearful of all the worst scenarios, Whitney pulled her hand away.

'Don't look so terrified,' Zach teased. 'At least try it on.'

'No!'

'Why not?'

Her mouth turned rueful.

'I might get to like it and not want to take it off.'

'Good. That's why I'm giving it to you, for ever.'

He was saying all the right words and

she wanted to believe this could happen, but everything conspired against them. Zach's gaze locked with hers and she wavered. Making decisions had never been impulsive for her. She always planned big stuff like this but Zach was sweeping her away. She needed to be sure. If she made the wrong choice and hurt Zach, she'd hate herself for life.

'Wear it as a dress ring,' he suggested gently.

Before she could hide her right hand, Zach slid the ring on to its third finger. The pearl's lustrous gleam mocked her. The showy diamonds glittered and the gold band reflected its richness. Whitney stared at it. Normally, she wasn't a jewellery person but the beauty of this exquisite piece stole her breath away. For now, this was as far as she could go, as much as she was prepared to concede.

Just when Whitney thought the pressure was off and she had claimed a reprieve, Zach said, 'How about twenty-four hours to make a decision?'

Whitney gasped, 'One day!'

'We could know each other for years and still not make it, or we could plunge in now and live happily ever after. Commitment doesn't come with any guarantees.'

'I need more time. Maybe I'm just a coward.'

'Let's have a coffee.'

'No. If you don't mind, I'd rather go home.'

'Really?'

She grinned.

'No, but I'm going anyway.'

Zach frowned and pulled her into his arms.

'I want to spend for ever with you.'

Whitney laughed.

'Don't look so injured. If I stay here, you'll cloud my mind and I'll never think clearly.'

The yearning to stay was strong but somehow she resisted. In reluctant acceptance, Zach pushed a hand through his tousled hair.

'I'll call a taxi.'

Within ten minutes, she was back at

her flat. As she climbed the outside stairs, Whitney knew that the newfound intimacy with Zach had irrevocably changed their relationship beyond the point of no return. She gazed down at the ring on her finger. Its meaning exhilarated yet terrified her.

The flat was quiet but she headed straight for bed.

Next morning, she saw the note stuck to the refrigerator in the kitchenette, telling her that Maz had gone earlier, for the day. Whitney moaned. She longed to talk to someone, do something, go somewhere.

In her bedroom, Whitney removed the ring and slipped it back into its box. Hidden away, it delayed the need for a decision. She took a long shower. Her thoughts recapped the past wonderful week with Zach — their first meeting; all the flowers; the picnic lunch in the limo; falling asleep in his arms; dinner in Sydney. As she dressed and brushed her hair, Whitney realised that Zach had become her whole world.

Unfortunately, one memory haunted her — the dinner last night at Winsmere. Clearly, the Chandlers had already cast their vote against her and it troubled her that she might be the cause of a rift between Zach and his family. Restless, Whitney made coffee, curled up on the sofa and stared at her compact sitting-room filled with flowers, which only reminded her of the giver and his proposal. Was she naïvely hoping for a fairytale ending that would never be?

She wandered downstairs into the shop and sauntered around, lovingly running her hands along the leather-bound spines of each cherished volume. She'd spent a decade learning this business, experience she would take with her when she moved on, which seemed inevitable. All the same, nostalgia and reality hit hard when she acknowledged that her secret dream to own this place one day would probably never come true.

Whitney stared at the phone on the

counter. Time to clutch at a straw. She picked up the receiver and dialled her father in Coober Pedy. As always, Mac was delighted to hear from his favourite girl, as he called her. The fact she was his only girl made Whitney smile. They chatted for a while before she explained her opportunity to buy the bookshop.

'You're welcome to every cent I've got but it won't be enough to help you. I'm sorry, honey. I wish I could help.'

He merely confirmed what Whitney already knew. He made a living opal mining but loved playing cards and gambling too much. He rarely stayed solvent for long but she loved him dearly. He was family and it had been worth a try. Whitney frowned to herself, her elbows resting on the counter as she looked out into Collins Street.

'It was just a dream if the business ever came up for grabs. I didn't think it would be this soon,' she told him.

He apologised again. Her father was a softie and she adored him.

'You sound a bit down, honey,' he went on.

She wanted to blurt out about Zach but checked her need.

'I'm fine.'

They chatted a while longer then hung up. Unsettled, Whitney made another call then returned upstairs. Her mother had agreed to meet her at the flat in an hour. Punctually, her taxi pulled up in front of the bookshop. As Laura paid the driver, Whitney watched the smartly-dressed woman in tailored slacks and a cotton jumper, wondering why she had never divorced her father and found another man. At fifty, she was still slim, her greying hair well cut, and she certainly didn't look her age. Whitney had inherited her mother's height and slender grace, her father's blue eyes and sandy hair.

Laura hugged her.

'What a lovely surprise to get your call.'

Whitney linked her mother's arm.

'Lunch on Southbank?'

They strolled along Collins Street, eventually crossed the Yarra River Bridge, sauntering along the cosmopolitan esplanade of shops and cafés thick with people dining beneath canvas awnings. They chose one of the main alfresco restaurants, seated themselves and ordered from the menu.

Edgy as she drank her wine, Whitney came directly to the point about the bookshop opportunity and her lack of finance, but her mother's response, too, was as expected. Laura apologised, unable to help. Like Mac, she offered money but it fell far short of what her daughter needed.

'Have you tried the banks?'

'Been there. Done that. I've no collateral, no money.'

Laura now expressed concern over the future, but her daughter dismissed it. When their salad arrived, Whitney played with her food.

After a while, Laura said quietly, 'What's his name?'

Whitney's glass of wine stopped

halfway to her mouth. She shouldn't have been surprised. Although Laura remained on the perimeter of her daughter's life, she remained perceptive and impartial.

'Zachary Chandler.'

Laura's green eyes registered instant recognition.

'The Winsmere Chandlers?'

Whitney nodded, well aware her mother was impressed. In the jewellery boutique, she thrived on the contact with the city's social élite. She stopped eating, carefully settling down her knife and fork.

'How extraordinary. I've met him in the boutique. How did this happen?'

Whitney shrugged.

'He came into the bookshop.'

Laura dabbed her serviette over her lips.

'You didn't mention him last time we met.'

'I didn't know him two weeks ago,' Whitney admitted.

Laura graciously concealed her surprise.

'Rather sudden, isn't it?'

Whitney smiled.

'Déjà vu, isn't it? Like you and Mac.'

Laura gazed distantly across the river.

'Yes.'

She took up her cutlery again and eyed her daughter.

'You're in love?'

'Yes.'

Whitney caught her mother's nostalgic gaze.

'Does he love you?'

'Yes, and he proposed last night with a fabulous ring.'

Laura's face and eyes lit up with recognition and astonished pleasure.

'Diamonds and pearls?'

Whitney nodded and gave a wry grin.

'Don't get too excited. I said no.'

Laura raised her eyebrows in silent question. Whitney sighed.

'We're from different worlds, like you and Dad. There's so much against us. What if Zach and I don't make it, either?'

Laura eyed her daughter.

'Whitney, you should know that Mac and I . . . ' She paused to sip her wine. 'We were never in love.'

Surprised, Whitney gaped at her mother.

'What! Never?'

'For six glorious months, Mac and I shared a fabulous passion, but never love. Each time before he returned to the outback, he begged me to go and live with him. But it was never a possibility for me, and there was no way he could live in the city. Look at me, Whitney. My clothes. Me. I'm a city person and he hated it here. He was like a caged animal.'

'Yet when you told him you were pregnant, he stood by you.'

Laura nodded, smiling fondly.

'He always had a heavy sense of duty. He insisted on supporting us.'

Laura sought Whitney's hand, and she thought her mother's eyes glistened with tears.

'Crazy thing is,' Laura admitted, 'I'd

do it all again. You're a special gift from a brief and wonderful time in my past. But neither Mac nor I would give up our lives for the other because we didn't have true love. If we had, I'm sure it would have made all the difference and we would be much more than just old friends.'

'Does Dad still care about you?'

'I believe so. Never deny your feelings, Whitney,' Laura said earnestly. 'Sometimes all we have to guide us is our instinct.'

They sat in the sun a while longer until Laura made her excuses and rose. She hugged Whitney fondly, begged to be kept informed and left. Absently spooning up the froth from her cappuccino, Whitney mulled over her mother's words. Love was enough for most people and she believed it could be for her and Zach, except for one major hurdle — his parents' disapproval.

Yet marriage was a decision only she and Zach could make. He was sure and, deep down, all obstacles aside, so was she. Whitney sighed. She had to take the plunge and trust her feelings, put her heart on the line. She never imagined choosing the love of her life would be this difficult. She finished her coffee, paid the bill and strolled back across the river.

7

Back at the bookshop, Whitney fumbled to unlock the door. She flew inside and snatched up the phone, her heart hammering with excitement as she pressed Zach's number.

'Are you sitting down?' she asked when he answered.

'Good news I take on my feet.'

'Then you won't need a chair.'

'I love you, Whitney Leighton.'

His deep voice was so soft, tears of happiness misted her eyes.

'We're going to make each other very happy,' he added.

'Never stop loving me,' she whispered. 'That's all I ask.'

'That will not be a problem, I promise. Are you wearing my ring?'

'Oh, no!'

Whitney laughed, wiping away her tears. She dropped the phone, ran upstairs, took the ring from its box and slid it on to her finger. Then she picked up the extension.

'Well, it's official. We're engaged,' she announced.

'Good. Don't take it off. You're mine for ever. Dinner here tonight?'

She sighed over the thought of a private, romantic dinner.

'Yes, please.'

Later, as she dressed, Whitney anticipated the intimate evening ahead, the plans she and Zach would make. It would be a small church or garden wedding at some vague and hazy time in the future. Whitney wanted to slow down and get to know Zach better. And she steadfastly refused to contemplate his parents' reaction.

She zipped up her loose black slacks, pulled on a soft jumper and, for a touch of class since it was a special occasion and it perfectly matched the ring, added her pearl necklace. A taxi then whisked her through the city to Zach's penthouse and he had barely welcomed and ushered her inside, before he pulled her into his arms and stole a long, breathtaking kiss.

'How's the future Mrs Chandler tonight?'

'I haven't thought that far ahead.'

'We should.'

'Don't be impatient,' she teased.

'There's no reason to wait, is there? Not backing out on me?' he added.

Whitney sensed concern behind his light-hearted manner.

'Of course not.'

In the dining-room, a small, round table had been set for two, already lit by red candles, matching serviettes and white china. A serving trolley held domed silver dishes. Zach caught her surprised look.

'I had it catered. I want to spoil you.'

Whitney would have been happy with baked beans on toast but saw his indulgent smile. Later, out on the balcony after they had dined, they danced to slow music under the canopy of a million stars.

'I wish this could last all night,' Zach murmured. 'But I'm expecting some-one.'

Whitney concealed a stab of jealousy and disappointment.

'Business?'

He pulled back to look at her and grinned.

'A surprise.'

'Your parents?' she quipped, feeling nervous but intrigued.

Zach laughed but wasn't drawn to explain. As if on cue, the doorbell rang and they moved indoors. He indicated one of the chairs in the lounge.

'Make yourself comfortable.'

He answered the door with a warm greeting.

'Rosemary, good of you to come at such short notice.'

'Zachary, darling, it's my pleasure,' came a slow, sophisticated drawl.

He introduced the ladies to each other. Still none the wiser and forcing herself to be gracious, Whitney rose and smiled. She noted the woman's smart red designer suit, long red nails and black perfectly-groomed hair.

'Firstly, my congratulations to you both. You have my absolute discretion until the formal announcement,' she said, sitting down on the couch. 'Has Zachary told you why I'm here?' she asked Whitney.

'No.'

With an amused glance at both of them, she said, 'How romantic,' then she turned again to Whitney, saying, 'I'm a wedding planner, dear.'

Whitney was stunned. She was probably supposed to be surprised and delighted but instead felt hurt at not being consulted. And so soon? Perhaps this was how Society did it. Noticing her confusion, Zach reached across and clasped her hands in his.

'This is an initial consultation. Rosemary will acquaint us with the process and discuss ideas. Ask for whatever you want. She will arrange it.'

'I just want you,' Whitney breathed, holding his gaze, suddenly feeling overwhelmed and superfluous.

'Oh, how sweet,' Rosemary gushed, and then unsnapped the lock on her bag, retrieving a thick, leather diary and flipping it open.

'It's never too early to start planning. This will be the wedding of the year,' she addressed Zach.

Whitney gulped down her dismay and glanced at Zach.

'We haven't told our parents yet or discussed it.'

Zach slid an arm about Whitney's shoulders.

'You don't need to worry about a thing. Rosemary will do it all for us.'

'Well, let's get started,' Rosemary bubbled.

Whitney swallowed hard. How did she tell Zach tactfully in front of Rosemary that this was not what she wanted? For the simple ceremony she had in mind, all this fuss hardly seemed worthwhile.

'I'd rather enjoy planning our own wedding,' she hinted, to no avail.

'You can still have everything you

want,' Zach said. 'Just pass on all your ideas to Rosemary.'

'I have a list. We'll check off each item as we go, shall we?' Rosemary enthused.

Glancing between Zach and Rosemary, Whitney decided to see what they had in mind.

'Now, we need a date.'

'As soon as possible,' Zach replied.

'Not for a while,' Whitney said at the same time.

Rosemary pulled a tactful smile.

'Are we thinking weeks or months here?' she asked.

'Weeks,' he said.

'Months,' she said.

The future bride and bridegroom stared at each other.

'We'll negotiate.'

Zach turned on a warm smile.

'This isn't a business deal. It's our wedding,' Whitney said tightly.

Aware of the conflict and endeavouring to smooth over it, Rosemary bustled on.

'Well, let me know the moment you decide. Now, about the venue. St Paul's, I presume?'

Zach nodded.

'Cathedral?' Whitney gasped.

Rosemary scribbled furiously in her book then looked up.

'Number in the wedding party?'

Whitney shrugged.

'Tess and Maz.'

'Only two?' Rosemary queried bluntly.

'Victoria and Caroline each had six. You can have as many as you like,' Zach offered generously but Whitney stood firm.

'No. Thanks all the same. I just want my best friends.'

'Colour scheme?' Rosemary pressed on.

Deciding to play along, Whitney said flippantly, 'Black and white stripes.'

Zach tensed beside her, apparently wise to her charade, so she didn't risk looking at him. She barely managed to keep a straight face as Rosemary blinked, covered her initial shock, and then beamed.

'I can work with that.'

Fearing the proceedings would degenerate into a farce if they continued, Whitney mustered courage and rose.

Glancing down at Zach, she said, 'I'm sorry,' then she addressed Rosemary. 'Until we have firm decisions, I suggest we don't take up any more of your time, especially on a weekend.'

'But, Whitney, dear, we've only just begun,' Rosemary stammered. 'Zachary?'

Remaining tactfully loyal, Zach rose beside her.

'Whatever Whitney decides,' he agreed graciously, then led Rosemary to the door as she hastily stuffed folders and pens back into her huge bag.

Whitney awaited Zach's return.

'Whitney?'

Fearing their first argument, she faced him.

'You should have consulted me. Inviting Rosemary was premature and inconsiderate. We only met last week. You proposed yesterday. I accepted today and already you've arranged a wedding planner. I can't do it this way.'

Scowling with concern, Zach moved closer and took her hand.

'I didn't mean to rush you. Whitney, honey, I just want you in my life as soon as possible. I assumed you wanted the same thing. Let's talk about it.'

He reached out for her but she shook her head and pulled away.

'I'm tired. It's late.'

Frowning, he said, 'All right. I'll come down in the lift with you.'

'No, please. And thank you for dinner. It was memorable.'

'May I see you tomorrow?'

'Possibly.'

Her hesitation obviously bothered him.

'I'll call,' he said.

Whitney tossed and turned all that night, failing to sleep. Miserable and worried, she wondered if she and Zach really were right for each other. In their haste, had they made a mistake? She punched her pillow, rolled over and tried again. She had just begun to doze, when the telephone rang.

Sleepily, she picked it up.

'I love you.'

Whitney sat up in the darkness.

'What if Maz had answered?'

'Did you hear what I said?'

'Yes. Why did you call?'

'I promised.'

Whitney frowned at the glowing red numbers on her digital clock.

'At this hour?'

'I couldn't sleep. Whitney, about Rosemary. I'm sorry. I thought you'd be excited. I jumped in. I was wrong. I'm used to making decisions alone. I didn't think. It won't happen again.'

Whitney closed her eyes, tense from the desperation in his voice.

'Thank you. Apology accepted.'

'Big mistake, huh?'

She grinned in the dark.

'Huge.'

'I want to be with you all the time and the only way to change that is to marry you. Fast.'

Zach sounded so unhappy and repentant. Whitney sighed with relief.

Everything would be fine. This was just a hiccup. They would make it.

'If you're not sleeping, what are you doing?' she yawned.

'Sitting out on my balcony in the dark.'

'And?'

'Talking on the mobile to my fiancée.'

'Keep talking.'

Whitney pictured him, and snuggled farther down under the bed covers.

'Wishing you were here with me.' His voice lowered. 'Lunch tomorrow?'

'I'm working,' she replied, loving hearing his voice so close.

'I thought you wanted to talk.'

'I do.'

'Then I'll see you for lunch.'

'All right.'

'Alexandra Gardens along the Yarra?' he suggested.

She agreed and they arranged a meeting place.

'I'll bring lunch,' Zach offered, then hung up.

Whitney snapped out the light and slid beneath the covers.

8

Whitney deliberately arrived early in the gardens next day for lunch and watched for Zach. Within minutes, he appeared, swinging a picnic basket, a tartan rug slung over his shoulder. At times, he still seemed like a stranger to her, but a stranger she loved. When he caught sight of her, he smiled and waved and her heart tumbled with joy.

He paused a step away from her. Because he looked so awkward, Whitney leaned forward, kissed him soundly and lifted the hamper lid.

'What's in here?'

He relaxed.

'Everything.'

'Good. I'm ravenous.'

They opened the rug, stretched out across it and unpacked the food. Zach uncorked a bottle of wine and they began to eat, feasting on cheeses, shaved slices of ham and salmon, crusty bread, chilled pâté, melon and strawberries. Zach looked at Whitney cautiously.

'We only have an hour. You first.'

'Promise me in the future we'll always discuss things and make our decisions together,' she began.

'Done,' he agreed quietly.

'I know you're in a dynamic business. You're in charge and have to make snap judgements but I'm a simple, working girl. I don't expect everything to be grand. Less is more, if you get my drift.'

'I'm impatient.'

'And I'm not a share transaction to be dealt with while the market's hot. We're talking long-term here. At least with me, you're going to have to slow down. And,' she added, 'we need to tell our parents.'

Zach shrugged easily then replied, 'I'll tell mine. You tell yours.'

'Shouldn't we do it together?'

He considered her suggestion.

'How about an official engagement dinner next week at my place with both families after we've told them?'

'Mac and Laura will be a cinch but yours won't be quite so smooth.'

'I'm accustomed to their disapproval.'

'Want to discuss our wedding now?' he prompted.

She liked the way he put it, their wedding.

'Not with Rosemary.'

'We're both working full-time. It will ease the pressure of organisation,' he said persuasively.

'How hard can it be? Book a church, minister, flowers, send out invitations and show up on the day, more or less.'

'You want something small, don't you?'

'Personal, yes.'

'Mother will be speechless. She'll want a cast of thousands.'

'Is that what you want?'

Zach's gentle gaze was full of love.

'I don't care how we do it. I just want to marry you.'

Why was today so easily falling into

place when last night had been an endurance? Whitney leaned across the basket between them and brushed her lips over his cheek.

'Don't become too agreeable. Stay a challenge.'

She combed her fingers through his hair. He was so adorably gorgeous, her heart burst with love for him. She cupped his face in her hands and kissed him again. Zach's mouth trailed over her chin and along her throat.

'Let's get married in two weeks.'

Whitney's half-closed eyes widened.

'You're doing it again!'

'We love each other. Why wait?'

The wind gusted and scudding black clouds loomed overhead.

'I don't believe this.'

Whitney's upturned palm caught the first drops of rain.

'We still have half an hour. My apartment's close by.'

Whitney nodded and closed the hamper. Zach held the rug over their heads and they ran for a tram.

While he made coffee in the apartment, Whitney watched the heavy spring shower drift in sheets across the city. Already, the sky had lightened in the west and the sun would soon reappear. They settled into the deep sofa together and Zach produced a large photo album, flipping through it.

'This is Caroline's wedding to Walter Bailey. He's an accountant, the one who collects books. They have three teenagers, Thomas, Clare and Alice.'

'I'm looking forward to meeting them all,' Whitney said.

'Chandler children aren't usually included in formal, family functions.'

'Why ever not?' Whitney said, appalled.

'They're expected to be seen and not heard.'

'Well, they're hardly children any more. They're young adults and I think we should invite them.'

Zach grinned and kissed her nose.

'They'll be delighted.'

'Is this your other sister?' she asked as Zach turned more pages.

'Victoria. She made her début then disappeared overseas for ten years.'

'Caroline conformed but Victoria didn't?'

'Exactly. Victoria studied French and Italian at school, obviously with a plan in mind.' He chuckled. 'She worked in Paris as a waitress while she studied art. She returned to Australia, met Charles within a week and they married within months.'

'Do all Chandlers do things in such a hurry?'

'Not always,' he murmured. 'Some things are much more enjoyable when they're done very, very slowly.'

Whitney grew warm at his suggestion, then he proceeded to kiss her in such a manner that the album, forgotten, slid from their laps. They broke apart and rescued it, laughing.

When they settled down again, Whitney said, 'Charles looks distinguished.'

'He's a barrister with a passion for gardening, and Victoria is a talented artist. They have two toddlers, Alexander and Elliott, and a baby, Sophie.'

'Will they all come?'

'Definitely, to put you under the microscope,' he teased.

'Oh, dear,' Whitney sighed then quickly counted on her fingers. 'That makes fifteen. We could serve a buffet,' she suggested.

'Great idea.'

The sun announced its return by slashing golden beams across the penthouse carpet. Whitney stretched from her cosy position snuggled next to Zach and looked down over the damp, glistening city below.

'I must get back,' she sighed, without enthusiasm.

Before she left, Zach somehow convinced her to give Rosemary one more try. Whitney yielded but only because she had wildly agreed to be married in fourteen days. As Zach so smoothly argued, professional expertise would save them time and alleviate unnecessary panic.

In excited disbelief, Whitney rode a tram back to the bookshop. Good heavens, she would need a dress!

Her mother was ecstatic when Whitney phoned that night with news of the engagement and eagerly accepted her daughter's invitation to dinner at Zach's penthouse on Saturday night. Mac's reaction was quiet pleasure.

Whitney held her breath and asked if he would come to Melbourne to give her away. She released a long sigh of relief when he agreed. When he told her he would arrive the day before the wedding and leave the day after, Whitney smiled. At least he was coming but she was disappointed he wouldn't be at the engagement dinner. She hadn't really expected it but, where Mac was concerned, one always hoped.

Maz squealed and Tess burst into happy tears when Whitney told them, and they eagerly agreed to be brides-maids. They gasped, however, when Whitney told them how soon.

The following day, leaving their

emergency temp, Susan, in charge of the bookshop, the trio scoured bridal boutiques. As Whitney tried on gowns, the reality of her situation finally registered. She would be Mrs Zachary Chandler. In rare moments of privacy in the days that rushed her towards the altar, she practised writing her new name on scraps of paper and decided it had a distinctive, pleasurable ring.

Any precious time Zach and Whitney managed to steal away together was spent planning their family engagement dinner at the weekend, and a wedding the weekend after that. Neither had time to ponder the whirlwind decision. Even Whitney's doubts about marrying a Chandler were pushed to the back of her mind.

Wednesday evening, she and Zach met Rosemary again, this time with smooth success. Three hours later, Whitney flopped down on to the deep, luxurious sofa, kicked off her shoes and stretched out, exhausted.

'Thank heavens Rosemary thrives on

a challenge. Next, is shopping for dinner Saturday night,' she said. 'Why don't we set up a special table out on the balcony for the young people? They'll be close enough to keep an eye on, but far enough away to give the adults privacy indoors.'

'Aren't you the clever one? You see, I'm not just marrying you for your body. I'm after your brains as well.'

As much as she anticipated the party, Whitney was also awed by the prospect of meeting a barrage of future in-laws and relations for the first time all together.

'What will we feed them?'

'I'm good at pasta.'

Whitney chuckled and playfully nudged him in the ribs.

'Anyone can do that. Wait, do you have some really large saucepans?'

'What on earth for?' he muttered.

'Your pasta idea has got me thinking. We could make different sauces, put them all in big bowls and let them help themselves.'

'Come on,' Zach said seeing she wouldn't be distracted and helping her to her feet. 'I'll show you the kitchen. I warn you, though, that apart from pasta, I can't cook,' Zach admitted.

'I'll teach you.'

'We could hire a caterer,' he suggested.

'We could, but we won't, will we? We agreed to do this together, remember? What will we have for dessert?'

'Let's buy two sinful gateaux from a specialist patisserie I know, and serve it in decadently thick slices with ice cream.'

'Sounds wonderful,' she breathed as their lips met softly.

Thursday and Friday sped by in a flurry of working, planning and telephone calls. Since their official announcement, a stream of Chandler family and society friends invaded the bookshop and Zach's apartment where she now spent a lot of time, drawn, Whitney was sure, by a combination of etiquette and curiosity. Both his apartment and her flat bulged with gifts. Whitney was amazed.

113

Friday evening, with Zach working late, Whitney raided the supermarket for pasta, herbs and groceries. She returned to her own flat to collect her new dinner dress, and then transported it all to his apartment in the limousine that Zach had placed at her disposal, thankful that she didn't have to struggle on a tram or pay for a taxi. Weddings were expensive and her personal funds low. The honeymoon she had left up to Zach.

To her delight, she met him in the downstairs lobby and he helped carry her load and unpack. Relieved at finally stealing time alone together, they dawdled over a scratch meal of omelettes, salad and wine. Afterwards, they ignored the washing-up and sank on to the deep leather sofa, losing themselves in the simple enjoyment of being together. They watched television for a while, and then Whitney dozed while Zach read newspapers.

9

Next morning, Whitney was at Zach's apartment before Zach stirred. She let herself in and called to him, opening his bedroom door.

' 'Morning, sleepyhead. Victoria Market, remember? I'll make breakfast while you shower.'

Whitney hummed in the kitchen as she whisked eggs and milk together, and heated the pan. He came downstairs smelling fresh and looking devastatingly handsome. They ate on the balcony, bathed by another burst of early spring sunshine, before setting out for the market.

They found a parking space near the Queen Victoria Markets on the city's northern fringe. Whitney and Zach joined the jostling crowds heading for the fresh produce stalls. He watched, amused, as Whitney selected and haggled for fruit, vegetables and massive bunches of flowers.

He leaned across and whispered, 'Price doesn't matter, you know.'

'Bartering is half the fun.'

Laden with bags, they struggled back to the car and returned to the apartment.

'Can you prepare lunch while I sort out the ingredients?' Whitney asked. 'Can you manage a ham sandwich, sliced fruit and a glass of wine?'

'I can pour wine.'

'Can you butter bread?' she teased.

'Probably.'

'There you go. You're halfway to lunch.'

Mid afternoon, the gateaux were delivered and stored safely in the refrigerator. By the time long shadows stretched themselves across the city, rich and tangy aromas emanated from the kitchen. Whitney had never seen Zach so enthusiastic and doubted he'd ever been so domesticated. While he stacked the dishwasher and tidied the kitchen, Whitney snipped and primped flowers into lavish arrangements all over the penthouse.

Early evening found her critically scanning everything — tables draped in crisp white linen, cutlery and glasses gleaming beneath soft lights, and the patio doors open wide to admit the night air.

'We've done well,' Zach said as he placed an arm around her shoulders.

'I need everything to be just right.'

'I know,' he replied and his deep voice soothed her tension.

An hour later, his appreciative gaze swept over her fitted light wool dress of stunning peacock blue. Around the high neck she wore the pearls.

'You're beautiful,' he whispered.

'I hope your family agrees.'

'Just be yourself and you'll charm everyone.'

All the demons of doubt that had plagued her over the past week dissolved with the single loving glance they shared, preparing her for the evening to come. Before their guests appeared, Whitney prowled the penthouse, checking her watch and the wall clocks, monitoring every detail and preparation.

'I wish they'd all just arrive and get it over with.'

She smoothed her hands down the sides of her dress, just as the doorbell chimed. Whitney's heart skipped. It was Laura. Her shoulders sagged with relief. Zach and her mother, as she already knew, had previously met in Caringfords so it was a mere formality that she reintroduced them.

Zach barely had time to pour them a glass of wine before the chimes rang again and the first of his family arrived. It was Caroline and Walter with their three attractive teenagers. Dramatic in black and dripping with heavy gold jewellery, Caroline's grey eyes were darker than Zach's and cold as steel. She spared Whitney the briefest glance, then headed for the bar.

Walter muttered something barely

audible but obviously polite and suitable, then trailed after his wife into the lounge. Their formality and stiffness made Whitney uneasy. She'd hibernate if the whole family were like this. Smiling rather more warmly than she felt, she beckoned to the three teenagers who were standing awkward and lost in the foyer.

'Follow me.'

She showed them the beautifully-decorated table out on the balcony.

'This is your dining-room for the evening.'

Thomas moved to the balcony railing.

'Wow. Neat view.'

'Haven't you been up here before?' Whitney asked.

Thomas shook his head. Having now encountered Caroline's aloofness, perhaps his mother had discouraged it, Whitney thought.

'You're welcome to visit Zach and me here any time you like.'

'Really?' Thomas said, genuinely surprised.

'Of course. He's your uncle. By the way, Zach loaded some new games into his computer in the study for you, and we've put a stereo system over there in the corner.'

Clare and Alice shared a polite, knowing smile and headed for the music. Thomas wandered off towards the study.

Indoors, Zach was greeting their latest arrivals. Relieved, Whitney found Victoria much more approachable than her older sister. Casual in slacks and a silk shirt, she had two toddlers clinging to her and she held a baby in her arms. Charles handed over a huge bouquet of freshly-picked, dewy flowers.

'These are for you,' he said and kissed Whitney warmly on the cheek.

Instinctively, she knew they were from his own garden and took pleasure in the genuine, unpretentious gift. Charles then handed a large box to Zach.

'And some vintage wine for you, old man.'

While Victoria bundled a sleeping Sophie upstairs, Whitney took Alex and Elliott by the hand and led them out on to the balcony. Clare and Alice seemed delighted to see them so Whitney left them to amuse themselves. Back in the lounge, a sullen Caroline drank and listened, and Walter brooded, but everyone else mingled and chatted.

Furious and despondent an hour later, convinced Zach's parents wouldn't appear, Whitney braced herself for the encounter with Everton and Muriel when they finally deigned to arrive. Whitney greeted them with a nervous smile. She tried to be friendly but coolness was all she could manage in the light of their rude lateness. What made it worse was their lack of explanation or apology. Breeding didn't guarantee manners, it seemed.

Everton's handshake was as domineering as Whitney remembered, probably in an attempt at intimidation or control. She forcibly withdrew her hand and ignored it. Muriel, remote and stylish in black and pearls, handed Whitney a crested ivory envelope and spoke matter-of-factly.

'Congratulations.'

The word was said as though she had won a prize, civil but curt, laced with bitter acceptance, as though she considered Whitney's engagement one of calculated triumph rather than genuine love.

'Zachary.'

She kissed the air beside his cheek as Whitney accepted the envelope, guessing at its contents, and suffered a wave of sadness at their treatment. She longed for their approval and acceptance into the family. As they moved away, Whitney overheard Everton's pointed insinuation to his son.

'This is all a bit rushed, isn't it?'

She stifled a gasp of shame. Zach's thunderous glare clashed with his father's. She saw his jaw clench and felt his body stiffen beside her as he drew her close.

With admirable control, he said, 'My fault entirely, I'm afraid. I'm impatient to marry her before she changes her mind.'

Thwarted, their attention was diverted by their grandchildren out-doors. Muriel raised her eyebrows and darted a meaningful glance at her husband.

'You invited the children?' she said with accusation.

'Isn't it wonderful?' Zach responded swiftly, smiling. 'All the family's together for once.'

His hint was not lost on them but their chill demeanour told him they disagreed.

'It's far too cold out on the balcony,' Muriel persisted critically.

No more than in here, Whitney bit back the retort on her tongue.

'They're having such a wonderful time, they don't seem to be noticing, do they?' she said pleasantly.

Whitney was appalled that she and Zach were forced to justify themselves on every count before such petty persecution. Why couldn't his parents simply be happy for them?

'You've done all this yourselves?'

Muriel's derogatory gaze now swept the apartment but her observation was not a compliment. If she had expected a formal dinner party she would be disappointed. Whitney no longer cared. Zach was right. Nothing would please them.

'Yes,' Whitney murmured, weary of being defensive.

'I'm surprised you didn't have it catered,' Everton said to his son. 'You're going to need a chef, Zach.'

'Am I?' Zach replied, dismissing the charge with a grin. 'Any more champagne anyone?'

Caroline sprang forward to refresh her drink which she had done repeatedly since her arrival, and greeted her parents with an obligatory, distant kiss.

Amazingly, as soon as Muriel approached Laura, they began chatting civilly to each other like old friends. Whitney sighed, thankful for at least one redeeming feature in the awkward proceedings. Escaping into the kitchen, she began transferring hot food into serving dishes. Within moments, Victoria appeared.

'Can I help?'

They exchanged a warm, conspiratorial smile and served the children first, settling them all down together outdoors. Then Zach lit the candles and announced dinner. Although Everton, Muriel and Caroline were clearly disdainful of the informal arrangements and initially held back from participating, everyone else wandered across to the kitchen servery, filled their plates and seated themselves at random around the table. Reluctantly, the others condescended to join them.

The meal, although enjoyed by the majority, continued with undercurrents and a brittle veneer. Whitney feared that it would always be so. In the face of Muriel's and Everton's open animosity, she despaired that they could ever become friends. Zach's parents would never accept his choice in marriage.

After the main course, Zach moved to help Whitney clear the dishes. When Victoria also rose to help, Caroline sneered.

'You really should have a maid, Whitney.'

'Should I?' she said, smiling lightly to hide her frustration.

The chocolate gateau was a hit with the children although they seemed equally interested in the gourmet ice cream. The adults helped themselves to dessert, except Muriel who refused and Caroline who fussed with a thin slice on her plate. Everyone else ate heartily and Whitney stubbornly returned for a second helping.

When delighted squeals of laughter floated in to them from the balcony, Caroline complained.

'Walter, control your children.'

'Let them have fun for a change,' Zach said with unusual sharpness.

With a stunned frown, his sister's mouth snapped shut.

Following dessert, Charles rose and

proposed a toast to the newly-engaged couple on behalf of the family. Although technically Everton's duty, it was embarrassingly obvious that he refused. Laura added her own good wishes and congratulations, then Zach made a brief response before inviting everyone to retire to the lounge for coffee.

As Whitney headed for the kitchen, she saw Muriel draw her son aside.

'Zachary, I thought you were virtually engaged to Melanie.'

Whitney grew still, awaiting his reply.

'You know that was never a possibility, Mother,' Zach replied.

'Your father and I had hoped . . . '

'That I would marry for love, as you did? I hope so,' he interrupted with cutting insinuation, then deserted her to mingle with their other guests.

Once the tense moment passed, Whitney released the breath she had been holding, shaking with nerves that the encounter had been so deftly handled by Zach. She set down her armful of crockery on the kitchen bench. Fortunately, Alice and Clare appeared, distracting her by groaning at the mountain of dishes stacked on the sink.

'I don't suppose anyone wants to rinse plates while I load the dishwasher?' Whitney quipped, not seriously meaning it, merely trying to keep a sense of humour under testing circumstances.

'We don't have to at home,' Alice pouted.

Whitney held her challenging gaze.

'It was a request, Alice, not a demand. Clare?'

After a moment, the younger girl shrugged, amused by the challenge and said, 'All right.'

'I didn't say I wouldn't,' Alice retorted and whirled from the room.

Clare turned on the tap and began rinsing. As Whitney took the plate, she noticed the girl's gaze constantly flicker to her left hand.

Eventually, she said, 'I love your ring.'

Whitney extended her hand for inspection and Clare sighed, then she blurted out, 'Mummy said your engagement is unfortunate. Why would she say that?'

Whitney privately cringed at the girl's innocent revelation.

'I guess it's because she doesn't know me,' she offered in charitable explanation.

'Well, I think it's romantic.'

'So do I. Your uncle's an extremely wonderful and generous man whom I love very much.'

At that moment, Elliott and Alexander scampered into the room and insisted they be allowed to play in water, too. Whitney lifted them up on to a chair, filled the sink with warm, soapy water and rolled up their sleeves. Then she supplied them with a handful of plastic utensils and bowls she discovered in cupboards and drawers, and left them to it. Feeling pleased by her small triumph in the kitchen, Whitney carried the coffee tray into the lounge, Clare trailing importantly behind bearing a crystal plate of patisserie biscuits. Zach was immediately at her side.

'Sorry,' he whispered. 'Got talking business with Charlie.'

'It's all right,' she said, looking down at her future niece. 'I had help.'

Some time later, the children were gathered together and the guests made movements to leave. Victoria and Charles with their young brood were the first to go.

'You're doing fine,' Victoria said and hugged them as they left.

'May I come and see you sometimes?' Clare asked Zach.

'Clare!' Caroline exclaimed, glaring at her daughter. 'I hardly think . . . '

'Of course,' Zach swiftly bypassed his sister's objection.

Muriel's only words as they left were, 'We'll be in touch.'

If every meeting was this unfriendly, Whitney wasn't sure she could endure it. Perhaps one became accustomed to coldness and apathy. Deliberately hovering in the background, Laura was last to leave.

'Well, that was an experience, wasn't it?' she murmured with a grin.

Whitney hugged her mother.

'Hardly the dinner party of the year but we coped.'

'Thanks for coming, Laura.'

Zach kissed her warmly on the cheek and his future mother-in-law blushed in a rare loss of poise. Whitney could only speculate how they would react when they met Mac. Like one of his polished opals, she hoped they looked beyond his rough exterior to the true gem of a man beneath.

The moment they were alone, Zach drew Whitney into his arms.

'I apologise for my parents' ungraciousness tonight.'

She swallowed back tense emotion. It had been difficult for both of them and it tore her apart.

'It's not your fault, but I hate being the cause of family hostility.'

'Life in the Chandler mansion was never smooth.'

With a mutual sigh of relief that the

evening was finally over, they climbed the stairs. Whitney had agreed to stay over in one of the guest rooms.

In the morning, she woke to find Zach had beaten her to it, and was already downstairs. He lounged on a balcony chair, reading newspapers, the sun gleaming on his dark hair. She hugged him from behind and he drew her head down for a kiss.

' 'Morning,' he murmured. 'I see your envelope from Mother is still sealed.'

Whitney noticed it on the table beside him on top of his pile of weekend newspapers.

'I'm not sure I'm game. What's in it?'

'Open it and find out.'

Cautiously she did so and from inside withdrew a cheque. She gasped in shock, staring at the obscene amount. With this much money, she could disappear to the south of France and live comfortably for life. In an ironic twist, it occurred to her that she could now afford to pay Mrs Pearce cash for the bookshop! She absorbed the incredulous possibility, excited, finally comprehending the power and influence of the world into which she was about to marry.

Whitney struggled with her conscience. The cheque was made out in her name alone, hideously generous and completely impersonal. Although ostensibly a joint gift, it reeked of blackmail. There was no card or note. In Zach's world, this was probably accepted and she determined not to fuss over it but felt sickened by its insinuation. Whitney imagined the perverse pleasure it would give her to tear it up.

To Whitney, the cheque almost signified buying her place in the family and the idea tarnished her amazement over the gift. Suppressing her stunned disbelief, Whitney slid it back into its envelope and frowned.

'Why is it only made out to me?'

'Family tradition,' Zach explained as he continued reading. 'Charles and

Walter got one, too.'

'You mean instead of affection? What am I supposed to do with it?'

'Spend it. Invest it,' he said warmly. 'You'll think of something.'

He appeared totally unconcerned.

'I do have one idea.'

'There you are, then,' he said and turned back to his newspaper.

Reeling with astonishment, Whitney topped up Zach's coffee, poured one for herself and pulled up a chair beside him, her mind dazed with possibilities as she sipped her hot drink. What should she do, Whitney wondered. Could she have it all? Owning Bygone Books was miraculously within her grasp but next birthday she turned thirty. Her biological clock was ticking and the years were slipping by.

Zach mentioned changes, and marriage was certainly that, probably the biggest one of all. The future would assume new directions and priorities for both of them. That motherhood might take precedence in her life was a possibility that had only surfaced in her mind last night. Whitney had found herself surprisingly broody at the sight of Victoria with Sophie, the baby. She sighed deeply and focused on the busy week ahead. The future would unfold and take care of itself, as it always did.

'Do you realise this is our last time alone together until the wedding on Saturday?' she said.

'At least we get to see each other at rehearsal Wednesday evening.'

'I have loads of shopping and dress fittings to get through. I need to pack up the flat and I promised Tess I'd go over the account books with her so she can manage while we're on our honeymoon. Are you sure we need to go away for a whole month?'

'At least.'

Whitney had protested when he first told her until she realised that it gave them four lovely, undisturbed weeks alone together. She studied Zach again. Everything would be all right, she was sure.

'Rehearsal was perfect, wasn't it?' Whitney murmured on the Wednesday night as she snuggled against Zach on the sofa back in his apartment. 'I can't believe your father came to the church this evening. Perhaps he's finally approving of me,' she quipped, hardly daring to hope.

'That reminds me,' Zach said abruptly.

Whitney was puzzled by his sudden businesslike change of mood. He reached across and took some papers from the inside pocket of his coat draped over a nearby chair.

'There's something you ... er ... need to sign.'

Whitney experienced a shadow of foreboding. She had seen his father draw Zach aside and pass him the envelope that he now produced. Distracted by rehearsals, she had forgotten about it.

'What is it?' she asked, her mind filled with dread.

'A marriage agreement.'

'I'm sorry?'

'A pre-nuptial agreement.'

Whitney gasped, staring across at the man she was supposed to marry in three days. A cold chill gripped her heart. All her hopes and dreams began to crumble. Her horrified gaze scanned the terse, legal paragraphs. Her grip tightened on the document and she lifted her gaze to face him.

'Is this the only reason Everton came to the church tonight? I thought he came because he was interested.'

'It's only a minor legality. It doesn't mean anything.'

Whitney grasped for a tiny sliver of reassurance.

'Then why ask me to sign it?'

'It's always been done in our family. It's just a formality, means nothing.'

Whitney saw from his puzzled expression that he had no idea of the crushing blow he had just dealt her emotions and pride. Indignation and anger boiled inside her. She scrambled unsteadily to her feet.

'You're wrong. It does mean something, Zach. It means you don't really love me at all.'

'That's not true!' Zach erupted, and to her amazement, Whitney realised her reaction had genuinely taken him by surprise.

'How dare you ask this of me? If you know me and love me, as you claim, you would know that you can trust me,' she went on.

'I agree.'

'You can't, or you wouldn't have accepted this.'

Deeply offended, Whitney thrust the papers back at him.

'Are you worried that I might have big ideas about your wretched money?' she accused bitterly.

'No!' Zach denied strongly. 'I don't think that.'

'Don't you?'

'No!' His voice softened. 'Whitney, it's only a piece of paper.'

'So you keep trying to convince me, but it's a very important piece of paper.

From where I stand, it's an extremely revealing, legal document. It lowers our marriage to a cold-blooded financial transaction. I expected our marriage to be based on mutual love and trust.'

'It will be.'

'Not if you expect me to sign that. You're assuming our marriage won't last. I gave you my unconditional love. I expected the same from you. If this is your parents' way of pushing us part, then it has worked.'

'But if you sign,' Zach argued desperately, 'it will prove to them that money means nothing.'

'That's the point. I shouldn't have to prove anything, nor you to me.'

Whitney could see by Zach's confused face that her reaction baffled him. Raised in a different world, he had no idea of the repercussions of what he asked. This was exactly what she had feared all along, something that would erupt to emphasise the social differences between them and challenge their love.

Miserable and deeply injured, Whitney conceded with alarming finality that Zach's request left her with only one possible decision. Slowly, she wriggled the engagement ring from her finger and placed it on the coffee table between them.

'I'm sorry,' she whispered. 'I can't marry anyone who doesn't even accord me basic trust.'

A shadow passed over Zach's stricken face.

'Whitney, I love you. I'll always want and need you,' he said in a low, tormented voice that wrenched at her heart. 'Please, change your mind.'

She stiffened herself against reaching out to touch him, an urge far stronger than her need to leave.

'Only if you destroy that document.'

'Whitney, my father's request is beyond my control. I'm his only son and major heir. It's his money he's protecting, too, not mine.'

'And you believe he needs to do that?' Whitney rasped out, horrified and on the verge of tears.

'He'll disown me if you don't.'

Whitney knew beyond all doubt then that their problem was hopeless to resolve. Zach was bound by birth and a lifetime of loyalty to his family. She had known him for only weeks. She could never ask him to choose.

'In that case, I'm sorry, Zach,' she said and almost choked on the words that she knew must follow. 'Consider our wedding cancelled.'

He caught her arm as she turned to leave.

'I'll speak to him.

Sadly, she shook her head.

'And change his mind? I don't think so.'

Before courage deserted her, she strode for the door.

'Whitney!' Zach commanded desperately from behind her.

She braved facing him. His stormy grey eyes glittered with implacable anger and pain. To distract her thoughts from how incredibly handsome the man was and how much she loved him,

Whitney focused on fact, not emotion, touched and heartbroken that his agony equalled her own.

'My wealth has been a problem for you since we met,' he was saying.

She knew it was true but not the issue here.

'I found it overwhelming that you're rich and I'm not, but in the light of that agreement, it appears it's also a problem for you. Trust cuts both ways.'

He let out a heavy breath and pushed a hand roughly through his hair.

'At least re-think your decision.'

'Are you prepared to do the same?'

Their gazes clashed in mutual misunderstanding and longing. For Whitney, the pull to stay was strong. If only he would rescind what he asked, she would be in his arms and they could begin again. Zach's jaw clenched. Just for a second, she thought he would change his mind. But he held up both hands in defeat and backed away.

Torn with heartache, Whitney realised he was letting her go. She forced her legs to take her through the door, closing it quietly behind her.

★   ★   ★

'Hi,' Maz greeted Whitney as she dried dishes in the kitchenette. 'Your wedding dress arrived.'

'Take it back,' Whitney snapped, striding past her friend.

In her room, she made two telephone calls before Maz appeared in the doorway. She stared as Whitney pulled a suitcase from her wardrobe.

'What happened? Where are you going?'

'Away.'

'Three days before your wedding?'

Remaining silent, Whitney wrenched clothes from hangers and tossed them toward her suitcase. Maz perched on the end of the bed.

'Don't ever marry a rich man,' Whitney exclaimed.

'Well, I wouldn't go that far. If one walked into my life . . . '

'They're pushy and dominating. Don't even think about it,' Whitney warned, shaking with anger. 'I feel cheap and small and unloved. I should never have agreed to this marriage.'

'What happened?'

Whitney glared at Maz.

'Zach and I argued, big time. End of story. The wedding's off.'

She hauled her case from the bed and checked her watch.

'Would you phone Tess for me and tell her to look after the shop?'

Maz threw her hands in the air.

'I don't believe any of this.'

'No need. This is my concern. I'm not flattering myself that Zach will try to contact me but in the unlikely event that he does, say I'm not in, please?'

Reluctantly, Maz nodded.

As Whitney swirled to leave, her gaze fell on the elegant ivory satin and lace creation hanging behind the door. She bit back tears. She'd forgotten how beautiful it was, and now she'd never wear it.

In the kitchenette with Maz at her heels, Whitney paused. She dropped her case and pulled her flatmate into a hug.

'I'm sorry. I've disappointed everyone. I honestly believed it would work.'

Then she lifted her case and ran downstairs. Outside, a taxi waited.

'Melbourne airport,' she told the driver.

She'd been lucky to secure a last-minute cancellation and astute enough to book it under another name. She needed time alone to wallow in misery and self-pity for a while, and lick her wounds.

During the flight to Adelaide, Whitney felt only emptiness and shock. Upon her arrival, already informed that there was no domestic service connecting with her final destination and having made the appropriate arrangements, Whitney winged her way inland on a private charter. It was still early evening when her small plane made a jerky touchdown on the rocky Coober Pedy airstrip.

Sagging with fatigue in the heat after a long day, she crossed to the small airport building, her footsteps dragging, her mind spinning. She phoned her father and waited. She hadn't seen him in over a year and hadn't bothered to tell him she was coming. When the big man arrived a short time later, it felt like coming home. His blue eyes lit up at the sight of her and his weathered face cracked into a grin. Whitney's heart filled with love at the solid, comforting sight of him.

She fell into his huge arms and he squeezed her tight. When they broke apart, she pulled back and sucked in a deep, steadying breath.

'The wedding's off.'

Mac didn't comment or criticise, he just spread one of his gigantic arms around her shoulders and carried her luggage to his battered truck. They rattled over the rough roads and pulled up in a cloud of dust outside his underground dug-out home. Many people lived in them because of the constant year-round temperature. They offered relief from the searing heat.

Whitney trailed wearily down the circular staircase after Mac into the neat white chambers below.

'Want to turn in?' Mac asked as he set her small case in the spare bedroom where she always stayed.

'I couldn't sleep. I'll join you in a minute.'

She needed to talk and knew he would listen. He planted a warm kiss on her forehead and left. Whitney had a quick shower then joined her father in the kitchen. He poured them each a beer.

'Come outside,' he suggested in is deep, gravelly voice.

Above ground, he pulled up two chairs and they sat beneath a clear black sky, overlaid with stars. The hum of petrol generators, used for electricity, mixed with distant laughter floated across to them on the still, night air. Tonight was chilly, but tomorrow would be hot again.

For the first time in weeks, she didn't feel rushed. Nothing could trouble her out here, except memories. Slowly, she began to talk, explaining how she met Zach, their whirlwind romance and the cause of their split.

'I've just lost my soul mate and the love of my life,' she whispered in agonising confession.

'What happened? What did you find out?' he probed.

'That Zach places other considerations before me.'

'Sometimes people have no choice.'

Whitney suffered a twinge of irritation. Mac was defending Zach.

'Zach wants to please his father, but I won't compromise.'

Mac drew on his cigarette and its tip glowed in the dark.

'Sounds like Laura and me. Can't live together, yet hate living apart.'

Whitney was amazed by his admission and indifference to her plight.

'You'll have to talk to Zach again,' he added.

Whitney squinted out into the night and stubbornly crossed her arms.

'Not unless he withdraws the agreement. If he won't do it because he loves me, then I don't want him.'

Mac finished his beer and enjoyed the last of his cigarette. From all appearances, he was taking her predicament rather lightly. Couldn't he see how important this was to her, and how serious? Knowing he would have more to say in his own good time, Whitney waited for it to come.

'Twenty eight years ago I refused to back down, too.'

'You don't ever seem to regret it,' Whitney observed.

'If we'd tried living in each other's world, we might have made it. We'll never know.'

Surprised at his nostalgia, she asked, 'You still care for Mother?'

'Some.'

Knowing Mac, that was an understatement. Whitney wondered why he'd never done anything about it. She expelled a long, slow breath. Mellowed by the beer and her father's harsh but soothing voice, her hurt eased to a dull ache and her head cleared sufficiently to think.

'Zach wants me to sign. I don't want to. How do we compromise?'

'Often you don't,' he drawled. 'Somebody gives in.'

'It's not that simple.'

'Didn't say it was.'

Whitney always marvelled at how Mac did that — communicated the biggest message with the least words. She mulled over his suggestion. The prospect of confronting Zach appalled her but she guessed it was inevitable. But giving in was unthinkable! Zach was wrong and she was right. The issue had been hurtful and revealed a complete lack of trust.

'Would it be so bad if you agreed?' Mac said over her thoughts.

'It sounds like you're on Zach's side,' she burst out. 'Whatever happened to family loyalty? And, yes, it would be awful and humiliating to sign that agreement.'

'It would prove your faith in him.'

'My faith in him? What about his faith in me? And how?'

'If you don't sign, you doubt him. Maybe you don't really love the man.'

'I do!'

'Even after what he asked of you?'

Whitney hesitated, then muttered unwillingly, 'Yes.'

'How much is your love worth? I'm not talking money. Can you bite your tongue and stop being so sensitive?'

'Why should it be up to me?'

'One of you has to make a move. Whoever does is the bigger person.'

'Zach should have mentioned the agreement sooner, or not at all.'

'You didn't give the man a chance to explain by running away.'

Mac made it sound like she'd quit on Zach when the going got tough.

'There's a difference between running away and getting away,' she replied sharply, offended he wasn't more supportive. 'Do you believe me or a man you've never met?'

'He can't be all bad. You were going to marry him.'

Mac stretched and rose from his chair.

'Sleep on it, girl.'

He dropped a kiss on top of her head and went inside.

' 'Night, Dad,' she murmured after him.

Talking with Mac hadn't gone quite as she'd imagined. She guessed he didn't agree with her stance because of his past with Laura. Whitney in turn wondered how she would view Zach in the future, with regret or fondness, knowing she would never remember him with anything less than the deepest love. But his cold-blooded request to sign the agreement had hurt.

Then Whitney thought of the mess she'd left behind for him — cancelling the wedding after Rosemary's tireless hard work; Laura's disappointment; Everton and Muriel's elation. Bitterness consumed Whitney that Zach's parents had won. She had played into their hands. She could have called their bluff and signed but that would have compromised her principles.

All this dissection and angst was getting her nowhere, she decided, and returned indoors. Exhausted, she fell asleep in her T-shirt and woke next morning to the sound of voices. In a haze of half awareness, she realised Mac was talking to one of his mates. Whoever it was, she probably knew him. Whitney stretched and sat up. She pushed a bunch of tousled silky hair from her face, scrambled from the bed and peered around the doorway into the kitchen. Her mouth fell open and her heart thumped in her chest when she saw the visitor.

How on earth had Zach found her?

10

At the sight of her ex-fiancé casually chatting to Mac like an old friend, Whitney's thoughts raced. She realised she must now face him. Yet she was also excited that he had sought her out.

Then her blood simmered when Mac mentioned her name and Zach laughed. This was more humiliation than she could bear. Heedless of decorum, she burst into the kitchen to confront them.

'When you're quite finished!'

Mac raised an amused eyebrow and Zach spun around, rising from his chair. His gaze melted her like warm syrup until she thought her knees would crumble. She eyed his handsome presence and inwardly sighed. Until she saw him, she hadn't realised just how much she missed him.

'What are you doing here?'

She tried to sound angry but her

question emerged as a mumble.

'I could ask you the same thing,' he replied.

Whitney glared at her father.

'Don't you have opals to dig or something?'

Unmoved, Mac finished his coffee. Exasperated by her father's stubborn refusal, she faced Zach again.

'Can't you cancel a wedding on your own?'

Addressing Mac, he said, 'This is going to take longer than I thought. Do you mind?'

Her father rose and left. Exasperated that he should co-operate with Zach and not his own daughter, Whitney wanted to hurl something at him.

'Coffee?'

Zach sauntered over to the pot and poured one, making himself at home. She shook her head and sank into a chair before her legs crumpled.

'I won't change my mind,' she said.

Zach set down his coffee, and rested his elbows on the table.

'I listened to you yesterday. Now you can listen to me. I love you, Whitney, above everything else in my life. I would do anything for you, give up anything for you.'

Her eyes pricked with tears. If he was softening her up, he was doing a fabulous job. That he meant it, she had no doubt. She just hadn't expected him to make such a passionate admission, a direct hit on her heart. He was playing mean and she struggled with her emotions.

'Despite what you think, possessions don't mean anything to me. I just happened to be born into a wealthy family. Regardless, I've worked hard and been successful on my own account.'

Absorbed, she couldn't run away.

'I won't apologise for being rich or ambitious. It's who I am. Everything I have, I earned. However,' he continued, 'I will apologise for my family. They're not easy people to know so you'll have to accept them as they are.'

Zach reached out and laid a warm, reassuring hand over hers.

156

'I realise you got the raw end of the bargain. Mac and Laura are far more human than my parents will ever be. But despite what you think, I beg you to trust me. That's what I ask.'

The touch of his skin against hers lowered her defences. Cautious, she pulled her hand away.

'I was trying until you pushed that document under my nose.'

'I know.' Zach's voice softened. 'I never dreamed you'd have a problem with it. I just assumed . . . I'm sorry. I had no idea it would offend you.'

Admirable sentiments, but it still left their dilemma unresolved.

'It still does,' Whitney said, meeting his troubled eyes.

Zach broke the eye contact, stood up and paced backwards and forwards. Then he looked back at her.

'Do you trust me, Whitney?'

She trusted him with her life. Surely he knew that. Whitney frowned, puzzling over the guarded manner in which he had asked. Strangely, thrown down like a challenge, she couldn't resist.

'Without reservation,' she replied.

During the long pause that ensued, she wondered what would happen next, until Zach produced a familiar piece of paper. Astonished that he would ever present the agreement document again, she stiffened and drew in a sharp breath. So this was the real reason Zach had followed her out here. Whitney eyed him in silent, stunned accusation, demanding answers.

In the light of his appearance out here, Whitney had assumed he wanted a reconciliation. She would have been prepared to compromise but if she signed the papers, it would be an admission that their love was fragile and unstable, and money the foundation on which it was based. The agreement lay on the table between them, innocent yet damning.

'The call is yours, Whitney,' Zach urged gently. 'Despite what you think, I promise you this document means no more to me than the trees cut down to make the paper and the ink used to print it. It's important to my father, not to me. You know I love you. You've just said you trust me. Please, sign it,' he urged softly.

On principle, she opposed the agreement and still smarted at the document's insinuation, but, when it came right down to it, all that mattered were her feelings, her love for Zach, feelings that gave her no choice. She faced the challenge and the undeniable look of love in his eyes. It all came down to this man and the two of them. Nothing else mattered.

Zach produced a personalised gold pen. Whitney hated herself for yielding and Zach for asking, but knew they must start anew somewhere. As Mac had so wisely said, someone must take the first step. She inhaled deeply, moistened her dry lips with her tongue and accepted the pen.

'Where do I sign?'

Zach's wide smile gave her heart wings. He shot around the table and swept her off her feet, Crushing her against him, he whirled her around with such enthusiasm she dropped the pen. Zach, in the meantime, fished in his shorts' pocket and produced her ring.

'Let's put this back where it belongs,' he said, sliding it on to her finger.

Whitney's lips met his mouth as her re-instated fiancé drew her into a long and passionate kiss.

'If you want to romance my daughter, Chandler, do it in private,' Mac muttered, reappearing. 'I'm an old man. My heart mightn't stand it.'

Whitney chuckled.

'You're as tough as old boots.'

Mac grunted and headed for the fridge.

'Guess this calls for a beer.'

He snapped open three cans and they clinked them together in celebration. Whitney's eye caught sight of the document still lying untouched on the kitchen table, taunting her. She tried to think of it as a formality, to accept it and appreciate the riches her husband brought to their marriage, knowing he possessed a richness far greater than money. Whitney caught Zach's gaze.

'Better rescue that pen,' she said looking at the floor.

Zach picked up the document.

'Mac?'

Whitney's father handed him a cigarette lighter and Zach held its flame to one corner of the document. Whitney's eyes widened in astonishment.

'What are you doing!'

'I just needed to know if you were prepared to sign.'

Whitney thought of all the anguish he had put them through to prove their love and trust for each other. She wanted to strangle him but how could she when she loved him so completely?

'What about your father? I can't believe he agreed to this.'

Zach shrugged.

'We all have adjustments and changes to make.'

She gasped, incredulous, wondering how on earth this fabulous man had achieved the unachievable. Whitney watched the paper singe to brown until the document was destroyed. Whitney was flooded with relief and happiness. She was going to be married after all.

Miraculously, Zach convinced Mac to fly back with them and by mid-afternoon they had landed back in Melbourne. Zach dropped Mac at his apartment and Whitney at her flat. Five minutes later, she joined Tess.

'You're back! Maz didn't say how long you'd be away,' her assistant beamed. 'I hope it was nothing serious.'

Whitney's mind scanned over the events of the last twenty-four hours.

'Small crisis, but everything's fine. I just have one phone call to make and I'll be right back.'

Upstairs, Whitney dialled the Chandlers' telephone number. She admired their generous concession over the agreement and felt it important to make peace before the wedding. She owed them that much at least. Who knows? They might even get to like each other. Finally, the phone was picked up at the other end.

'Mr Chandler? It's Whitney.'

'I'm listening.'

Whitney hesitated at his abrupt tone. She'd obviously caught him unaware but had expected a more civil greeting.

'I just wanted to thank you for changing your mind.'

'I beg your pardon?'

'About the pre-nuptial agreement.'

After a pause, he said in a clipped tone, 'I've done no such thing. Nothing's changed. Until you sign, Zach is no longer our son.'

11

Like a roller coaster, Whitney's heart plunged into shock and her excitement died as swiftly as it had risen only hours before. Her trembling hands replaced the silent receiver. Heartsick, she realised Zach had veiled the truth, letting her believe his father had conceded when all the time it had been his son who had given and lost the most.

The repercussions were unthinkable. Zach would be disinherited. How could any parent reject their child so callously? Didn't Everton and Muriel realise they would be the losers without their son in their lives?

Whitney frowned and sank into a chair. But Zach had said . . . She stopped and thought. What had he said exactly? Something about adjustments and changes, and that was all. And she had assumed . . . But, of course, that was precisely what Zach had wanted her to think. She ached with compassion for his selfless act. He couldn't do this. She wouldn't let him.

After the emotional high of this morning's reconciliation with Zach, Whitney despaired. Something had to be done. When she telephoned Zach's office, Whitney discovered he was in a meeting.

'Can you get a message to him? Ask him to meet me at his apartment in an hour, please. It's important.'

Whitney showered and changed into a stylish dark blue suit, one of the recent careful additions to her wardrobe necessary for her new life. She pushed her feet into high heels, carefully applied make-up and clipped on her pearls. With her hair neatly brushed, she grabbed a shoulder bag. Satisfied with her presentation in the mirror, Whitney decided she would do very nicely, gave her suit and jacket a final tug and hurried downstairs.

She cast Tess an apologetic glance.

'Trouble in paradise, again,' she muttered and strode out into the street to the nearest taxi rank.

Winsmere was as impressive in daylight as it had been floodlit at night. Its opulent grandeur and snobbish occupants only confirmed her resolve. As her taxi swept away down the impressive circular driveway, leaving Whitney standing beneath the Georgian portico, she pressed the doorbell.

A uniformed maid answered, eyed her curiously, ushered her inside and disappeared. Whitney hoped Everton's curiosity and desire to win intrigued him enough to receive her. Within minutes, the maid returned and led her across the marble hall into a sitting-room.

Expecting to meet someone, she found herself alone, finally resigned to their habit of keeping people waiting. After ten minutes, she drummed impatient fingers on her bag. At the sound of approaching footsteps, Whitney faced the door. Everton stepped courteously aside, allowing Muriel to precede him into the room.

'Everton, Muriel,' she greeted them with polite restraint.

Muriel sat on the opposite chair to the one she indicated to Whitney but Everton assumed a predatory stance in front of the unlit fireplace.

'State your piece,' he said, crisp and unsmiling. 'I'm busy.'

Whitney coughed and forced herself to look straight into his cold eyes.

'I love Zach and nothing will ever change that, not even your poor opinion of me. But I will not stand to see him deliberately crushed. You must change your mind. You cannot cut him out of your lives.'

The audacity of her blunt demand made her cringe.

'Must? Cannot?' Everton sneered. 'It's up to Zach.'

'On the contrary, it's up to you,' she challenged with quiet calm.

Whitney wondered if it was a twinge of pain or hatred that crossed Muriel's face. Everton glanced at his wife, not in consultation but with an aloof certainty that she agreed.

'Our terms are fixed. You sign or he's out.'

Adamant, he ground his jaw and glared.

Appalled by their cold-heartedness, reducing their son's worth to money, Whitney desperately pleaded with them one last time.

'Please reconsider, for Zach's sake. He's your son.'

'Was your cheque not large enough?' Muriel asked quietly.

An icy chill of repulsion made Whitney stiffen.

'It was too generous.'

'Free Zach and we'll double it. Get out of his life. Let Melanie back in.'

'He doesn't love her.'

'She's perfect for him.'

Whitney choked back the horror of his mother's crushing rudeness and blackmail. They truly believed she could be bought, that she was only attracted to their son for his money! How could wonderful, fun-loving, generous Zach be an offspring of this heartless pair? How on earth must he feel to have parents like this? Whitney's heart wrenched for him. So far, he had concealed his emotions. Inured to their insensitivity, it was probably a survival technique acquired over years of living with them.

With a burst of fresh determination, Whitney decided she would be Zach's family. She would make up for the one he had. She would give him all the love he would ever need, for ever, and, children, too, lots of them. She rose from her comfortable chair.

With a heavy heart and unconditional pity, she accepted their tyranny, hoping one day they bitterly regretted their cruel stance. She reached into her shoulder bag and removed the cheque. Slowly, she tore it into shreds, letting the pieces flutter on to the carpet at her feet. There had been hiccups in her whirlwind romance with Zach and doubtless over the coming years there would be many more but she wanted to start out their life together with a clean slate.

'If this is how you treat your family,' she said, filled with an empty calm, 'I'm surprised any of them is still loyal to you. Aside from acceptance and love, simple gifts that neither of you seem able to give, I can take no part of anything you offer, unless it's an apology.'

Feeling numb, Whitney turned around and strode from the house.

Walking along the leafy, opulent streets back to the main road gave her time to stop shaking and absorb the importance of the Chandlers' ultimatum. Her sickened heart endured deep guilt that she was the cause. Two days before their wedding, this was an unbelievable catastrophe. They could cancel the wedding and attempt to repair the damage between Zach and his parents, somehow try to resolve the issue and their differences but Whitney knew in her heart that was impossible.

She checked her watch. She was running late to meet Zach. She didn't have time for a tram so she hailed a taxi instead. Feeling washed out by the time she arrived at Zach's apartment building, she rode the lift swiftly to the penthouse floor. As the doors slid open, she caught Zach kissing an attractive, stylishly-dressed brunette outside his front door.

Doubt and jealousy hit her, but after the initial jolt, she frowned and moved forward. Zach would hardly arrange to meet another woman knowing his fiancée was due to arrive at any moment. It must be an unexpected visitor. She clung to the knowledge that he loved her, and approached them.

She returned his warm, intimate smile, all reservations forgotten. It was a bittersweet moment. Whitney was happy and in love, yet deeply distressed at the cost. The glamorous woman clinging to his arm turned. She leaned closer to him, whispered in his ear and moved from his side.

'Good luck,' she murmured as she strode past Whitney.

Instinctively, Whitney knew it was Melanie. Strong competition, she mused, as the lift door closed and the visitor disappeared from view.

'She's beautiful.'

'And ambitious. She wished us well.'

He slid an arm about her waist and planted a kiss on her lips. Perceptive of her every mood, Zach's smile faded.

'Are you all right?'

'I've just come from Winsmere. You weren't exactly truthful, were you?' she accused gently.

A look of embarrassed contrition crossed his face.

'You shouldn't have put yourself through it.'

'I had to try.'

'They told you the nasty truth?'

'Don't call us, we'll call you,' Whitney said regretfully then hugged him in comfort. 'They won't be at our wedding,' she said.

'No.'

'Or in our life.'

'Probably not.'

'You accept that?'

'I have to. They've given us no choice.'

'It's my fault.'

'Why? Because you're my choice and not theirs? It's done,' he told her softly. 'Let's move on from here, start afresh on our own, together.'

'But you may never have your parents in your life again,' Whitney protested, troubled.

'That's a risk I'm prepared to take. They may come around with time. Meanwhile, I can live without them. All I need is you. Until we met, I didn't realise how lonely my life was. You filled it with purpose and love. Besides, I can adopt your parents,' he added with an amused grin.

'They're both thrilled to have you.'

She appreciated his attempt at lightheartedness but knew he was hurting more than he revealed. He drew her against him.

'Good. Then let's just concentrate on our wedding.'

Because it held ten years of fond memories, Whitney dressed for her wedding in her tiny flat. She politely refused Zach's offer of the penthouse but graciously accepted a hired limousine to drive the entourage to church.

Following the family engagement dinner the previous Saturday night Zach had had an inspiration. His five oldest nephews and nieces were all invited to become members of the wedding party. What's more, they had all accepted. Whitney had feared Caroline would object but it seemed she conceded for this special occasion.

Now, thirty minutes before the ceremony and dressed only in a lacy slip, Whitney escaped the pre-wedding chaos of dresses, bridesmaids, hairstyles and flowers, and wandered downstairs to the bookshop. She trailed her fingers along the crammed shelves with their old editions.

She was gripped by only the briefest pang of nostalgic regret. It had almost been hers. She regarded its new ownership as an omen in her life, a change that was meant to happen, a sign that a new phase in her life had begun, that she must embrace it and move on.

'Whitney?'

Her flatmate's bright voice came to her from above.

'You're the bride. You're supposed to be getting dressed.'

With one last lingering glance, she returned upstairs. Whitney calmly accepted the fuss as Maz and Tess helped her wriggle into the dreamy wedding gown. Glowing with serene, motherly pride, Laura settled the veil around Whitney's face and the bride was ready.

Mac arrived looking uncomfortable in a suit, continually running a finger inside the neck of his shirt. Both parents exchanged meaningful glances and Whitney had no doubt they were happy to meet again after many years, reunited, if only briefly, by their daughter's marriage. At the sight of Whitney, Mac shook his head, speechless.

'I wouldn't give you away to a lesser man,' he muttered, hugging her.

'Don't be sentimental. You'll ruin my mascara. We'll visit,' she promised.

'With my grandchildren?'

'Perhaps,' Whitney said with a laugh.

He escorted her downstairs to the last in a line of four gleaming black limousines. The first three accommodated Maz, Tess and the flowergirls, dressed in pastel gowns, smiling and waving madly through tinted windows. As they were steered away from the kerb in front of the bookshop, Whitney glanced across at Mac. He smiled back and squeezed her hand.

Before they had travelled far, the car phone rang. Whitney raised her eyebrows and answered it.

'Where are you?' Zach growled, his deep voice impatient.

'I'm on my way. Don't worry. Where

are you calling from?'

'My mobile, outside the church.'

'Then hang up and get inside. I'll be there any minute.'

'You're worth waiting for,' he whispered tenderly.

Whitney hung up, smiling contentedly to herself over his thoughtfulness and inhaling deeply of the sweet, musky perfume from the ivory roses he had sent for her bouquet, exactly the same as those he had first sent her on that fateful day when a blustery early spring whirlwind had blown him into the bookshop and her life.

Ten minutes later, filled with a quiet sense of destiny and peace, Whitney stood poised in the entry of the small city church, her hand tucked securely into Mac's arm. She paused. This was really it. The church was magnificent with profuse bowls of huge white roses. Rosemary, ever the perfectionist, had excelled.

From behind, the bride felt a gentle nudge at her waist.

'Changed your mind again?' Maz whispered.

Whitney stifled a grin.

'No.'

'Then, in case you've forgotten, you're supposed to walk down the aisle, not stare at it.'

Tess giggled, then Mac, huge, blond and beaming with pride, urged Whitney forward for the short, sedate walk to the altar. As rousing organ music began to play, the ocean of guests' faces blurred and her gaze focussed on the man at the other end.

Zach, tall, distinguished and incredibly handsome, turned. His smile lit up the church. Her heart swelled with love for him and the happiness she knew they would share for life. She wanted to run into his arms but instead walked slowly and deliberately towards the man who, fate had decreed, would be her future, whatever it held.